The Dead Detective

The Barrel Full of Spirits

Jesse M Harvey

Books may be ordered through booksellers or at www.jessemharvey-books.com

ISBN: 978-1-956344-10-3 (Paperback)

ISBN: 978-1-956344-09-7 (ebook)

Cover design and formatting by: Books by E M Garner

Publishing House: Mighty Mama Mouse

Pen Name: Jesse M. Harvey

Contents

"The afterlife is whatever a soul wishes or believes it to be."
    - Aimee Carter

Content Warning

- Death of a child (off page)
- Murder and attempted murder
- Attempted rape
- Serial killer

Prologue

I'm Leroy Mahoney, of Bartley and Mahoney's Investigation Agency. That's been my gig since the winter of 1945. My office is still parked on 34th and Main Street. I count winks upstairs and grinds downstairs. It's a nice set up. Well, it was until I got fitted for a Chicago overcoat. I wasn't too thrilled to be taking a dirt nap, but I figured we all have to go sooner or later. What I didn't expect was what happened after I died.

See, like most folks, I didn't give much thought about what death was like. I was too busy living. I thought when it was over, the curtains closed, and the lights went out. I should have known it wouldn't be that simple. Being dead is as complicated as living.

The other side of the veil isn't static. The world in-between changes as the people do. It's not as solid as the land of the living. Each person who carries a belief on what the afterlife should look like affects the world to some degree. Probably the biggest effects are on the people who reside there. They are shaped and powered by the memories of the people left behind. Until those that die are able to let go of the mortal world and release their tethers, they are trapped in the in-between. That's where I come in. If you're dead and got a problem, I am the one you go to see. It's not glamorous sorting through the dirty laundry of a person's life or death. It can be messy and even dangerous, but that's the job.

Just because I'm dead doesn't mean I don't need to earn a living.

Chapter One

THE MIDMORNING SUN was completely blocked by the rain clouds, and the tall trees suffocated the narrow thoroughfare as the hired silver car followed the winding path along the secluded road. The polite driver that had picked Iris Porterfield up at the station had been graciously quiet since he started the car, and the interior of the vehicle was filled with a cozy quiet. The passing scenery helped soothe Iris's raw nerves, and she was finally able to relax against the backseat cushions.

Iris looked down at her phone with dread. She had it turned off before she boarded her train.

I need to check in with Randal. Just because they message me doesn't mean I have to answer. She held the words of her therapist firmly in her mind as she turned her phone back on. She let out a sigh of relief. There were only a few messages waiting.

They don't know I have left yet.

Brenden: You didn't answer. Are you ok? Call me.

Iris grimaced and quickly deleted the message. She took in a deep breath before she continued through the waiting messages.

Vanessa: Your mom called. I said we were having a girls' night. I didn't mention anything. But I think she knows. I will pick up your cat tomorrow. Stay Strong. YOU GOT THIS!

Iris smiled and quickly sent back a heart.

Mom: Hey Sweetheart. Call me as soon as you get this.

Mom: Your father is looking for you.

Mom: Brenden called. Did something happen? Call me.

Dad: Don't forget about the luncheon on Thursday. You and Brenden have to be there to meet the shareholders.

Iris swiped to ignore the messages from her parents.

Randal: Thank you for volunteering. This client has been with the firm for years. You are the third person we have sent. Do your best.

Randal: Jerry retired last month. I think he is in Palm Springs. PS I don't have a way to contact him, but I forwarded all the records to your server. Message me as soon as you can.

Iris: I arrived and was picked up by the client's driver. On the road now. I will let you know how it goes. I won't let you down.

Iris carefully typed out a reply on the phone before turning it to vibrate. Making the right impression was incredibly important in these situations. Wealthy, powerful men were very particular about who they let handle their money. As a female accountant, she already had to seem more professional than her male counterparts. It was a skill she had mastered early while working with her father and his business associates.

As they neared their destination, Iris went over her mental checklist. She checked her makeup in her small hand mirror. It was all done in complementary shades of nudes to be professionally pretty. Her dark-brown hair was carefully secured in a French twist at the back of her head. It wasn't easy to look professional when your features were more round cheeks than sharp angles.

Iris had learned at an early age that presentation was very important to those in positions of power and wealth. She had picked her outfit with care. It was tailored to flatter her short and curvy frame.

With no signs or designation, the car turned and drove up a long lane. Impressive ornate gates opened automatically, allowing the car to pull into the roundabout in front of the large manor. The heavy rains and gloomy sky did little to diminish the manicured lawns and meticulously kept grounds. The neat hedges and fine gardens were lovely in the dim light. The house, however, seemed oppressive in the delicate grace of the landscape. It was dark wood and heavy stones shaped into rigid, squared opulence.

Iris's blue eyes widened as she finally got a full view of the house. *It looks so dark and empty, like no one lives here.* There were no lights visible from inside the building. *Home* didn't seem the right word. It was a mansion, but there was nothing homelike about it.

The car came to a stop in front of the large double doors. With the grace that came from years of repetition, the driver exited the vehicle, unfurled an overly large umbrella, and opened her door. Iris pushed her nerves aside and disembarked onto the cobblestone drive, huddling instinctually under the umbrella. After closing the door, the driver led her to the protection of a small awning at the front entrance. Her well-turned heels clicked as she hurried to the front steps. He abandoned her there and returned to the car.

Iris took a moment to make sure her blue-grey suit was clear of any raindrops. She held her briefcase loosely in her left hand before she rang the doorbell. The door was answered so quickly she knew that they must have been waiting on the other side. Iris greeted the serious-looking woman with a professional smile.

"Good morning, I'm Miss Iris Porterfield. I was sent by the agency. I believe I am expected." She kept her tone confident and calm. Iris adjusted her glasses and waited for the serious woman to step back and let her in.

The woman looked her over for a long moment before finally nodding.

"Yes, please come in. My name is Julie Merulay. I am the main caretaker for Mr. Bartley. I am glad the driver found you alright. We appreciate you coming all this way." She moved, allowing Iris to enter before shutting the door.

The unusually heavy door echoed in the marble-floored foyer. Julie Merulay wore soft-soled white nurse-style shoes that squeaked slightly as she walked. Iris followed behind Julie and her squeaking shoes, walking softly by putting her weight on her toes so her heels were off the marble. The house was dim; only a handful of lights fought to dispel the gloom.

Iris passed through the large, open foyer and into what looked like a greeting room before they turned left. This carpeted hallway was much more reasonable in size.

At the end of the hall was a quiet, cozy study. Julie led Iris in, where she was greeted by a small warm fire that crackled in the oversized fireplace. The thick, ornately carved mantle was covered in small plaques and awards.

The built-in bookshelves were loaded with books. Iris

noticed that some of them were new releases. All were very clean, so either he read them frequently or someone dusted daily. Small stacks of books covered most of the tables, and though the rest of the house was dim, this room was filled with soft golden light. A perfect reading light for old, tired eyes. An elderly man rested in a large, wingback chair. He looked up as they entered, smiled, and rose slowly, setting aside his book on the end table.

"Ah, hello, hello. You must be Miss Iris Porterfield. Mr. Thursby assures me that you are the best he has to offer."

Mr. Bartley extended a hand. Without hesitation, Iris stepped forward and shook it. His hand was cool to the touch. Iris could feel how thin his skin was stretched over his bones, but his grip was strong. He motioned for her to sit in the chair opposite him.

She could smell his cologne, a faint mix of sandalwood and maybe bayberry. It was almost enough to cover the lingering scent of scotch and cigars—Mr. Bartley's vices of choice, if the empty tumbler and full ashtray on the side table were any indication.

"The pleasure is all mine, Mr. Bartley. You have a lovely home," Iris said in her carefully crafted, cool professional demeanor.

Mr. Bartley stood a full head taller than Iris even in her heels. He was lean in frame and well dressed in casual house wear. He was old enough to be her grandfather, with a full head of silver hair. Iris could see the boyish charm hidden in the wrinkles and lines of his face. At one point, Mr. Bartley had been quite the lady's man. Now, he seemed like a charming, happy grandpa.

Iris sat gracefully on the chair across from his wingback. She tucked her skirt under her stocking-clad legs that were crossed at the ankle. She sat very straight, being careful to keep her posture proper.

"My apologies for requiring you to venture so far to meet with me. I don't go into town anymore." he said as he sat back down. "Would you care for some coffee or tea?"

Iris shook her head and kept her smile. "No, that's quite alright. If it's alright with you, I would like to begin as soon as possible. I still have to go check in at the hotel."

She was relieved when he agreed. She kept tight control of her features and did her best to not let even a hint of her nerves or discomfort show. Years of practice and training helped her keep her calm. *As long as I keep control of the meeting, I will be fine.*

Mr. Bartley smiled and nodded. "Of course, of course. It's just been so long since such a lovely lady has come to visit," he said as he took a sip of the drink he already had next to him.

Iris did not respond to the compliment; instead, she lifted her briefcase into her lap, and with a practiced motion, she pulled out a specialized black folder she had made with the company logo embossed on the front. Little details like this made clients feel special. She kept her thoughts focused on what needed to be done.

"So, as I understand, you reached out to our company directly." She didn't actually look at the pages in the file. His information was there, but this was about showing him what she was capable of. "Someone has been stealing from you, and you wish to quietly discover who it might be?" She set down her briefcase and set the folder on her lap. "But you don't want us to report it to the authorities?"

Mr. Bartley seemed a little surprised by her speech. "No questions about how I know someone is stealing? What proof I might have? No subtle jabs about medication making me paranoid?" Mr. Bartley was staring hard at Iris's face.

Ahh, there it is . . . That's why he keeps asking for someone new. They didn't believe him.

"Mr. Bartley. I don't take jabs, and finding proof is my job. If you say your money is being stolen, I will figure out exactly where every penny of your money has gone and is going. My only question is, why not report it to the authorities once I find the proof?"

Mr. Bartley smiled softly over the rim of his cup. "Because I believe it is someone I love. I think my family is stealing from me, and if possible, I want to keep it 'in house.'"

Iris smiled softly and nodded. "Alright. If that is what you want, then that is what we will do. First, of course, we will be going over all the bank assets, funds, as well as the royalties and investments. Those can be done remotely; however, we will need an appraisal of the physical assets. This should include properties, collections, items of value, art, etcetera." She spoke in a carefully crafted tone. It was not too fast-paced but also not lingering. Clipped and carefully rehearsed from many similar meetings. She handed over documents for Mr. Bartley to review and sign.

"If you please, sign at the highlighted lines. I believe you were called by the law office. Mr. Thursby already sent them copies of these. When you have signed, please have them sent to your attorneys and they will forward them to us. The next step will be very simple . . ."

Mr. Bartley listened with a pleasant smile as he took the paperwork without giving it much attention. Instead, he spent the time studying the woman across from him. She was very pretty. Her skin had a lovely rosy-glow complexion. Her hair, a rich chestnut brown, was pulled back into some sort of twisted bun. She wore large, round glasses that helped bring attention to her eyes. She had a full lush figure that was highly complimented in her tailored suit. Her blue eyes were just one shade different from her outfit.

He considered her practiced speech. The way she spoke made it obvious to him that her ease came from repetition and training, not from some born talent for speaking. He imagined she was very shy. She didn't maintain eye contact and her facial expression didn't change fluidly. She was very good at hiding her emotions, but Eugene Bartley had always been good at looking past the surface.

She is nervous. He considered the possible causes. The manor itself was an intimidating place. If she had been a local, he might have considered it was caused by the rumors surrounding the house—the neighbors all thought the place was haunted—however, he knew she took the train in from the big city. Perhaps it was her boss that had stressed her out. She was the third candidate. He realized he was being persnickety, but the other two had just rubbed him wrong. *One was a charming asshole, and the other a condescending know-it-all. Of course, it could be that she is a fan. That always makes people nervous.*

He looked down at her shoes. *Those are a low heel, only about an inch or so high. She is a short woman but isn't using them to compensate. They have been buffed, trying to hide old scuffs. Her suit is fitted and of good material, but not an expensive name brand. This is a woman with an eye for details and is diligent. Randal said she was the only one that had noticed any of the suspicious activity in the accounts.*

"I have a very important question for you, Miss Porterfield." He grinned inwardly as the moment of panic hit her face. Nothing was better than the look on a person's face when he caught people off guard. He did so enjoy the drama of a good twist.

She recovered quickly and sat very still. "Yes, of course. What is it?"

He paused for dramatic effect. "Do you believe in ghosts, Miss Porterfield?"

He had expected either a confused or a generally concerned look, like he might be crazy, which he got most of the time he asked. He received neither.

Miss Iris Porterfield smiled softly and considered the question. "Yes, Mr. Bartley, but I don't believe they are relevant to this conversation." She turned to the paperwork and continued with her well-rehearsed script.

The Brownstone Agency had assured him she was their best accountant and appraiser. He needed a partner that could spot the details, think things through, and had a poker face just good enough to fool other people. Eugene smiled. *She will do very nicely.*

"Excellent! I look forward to working with you on this. I have been assured that you are one of their top appraisers . . . So, I am sure you will do fine . . .," he said quickly. He waved a hand and gathered up the papers she had been explaining.

"Julie!" he shouted down the hall, even though he knew she wouldn't be far off. He turned his attention back to Iris. "I will have Julie get you the key to the office on 34th and Main. That is the original office that my partner and I started in. After he passed, I kept working out of it. I was never the investigator he was, but when my books took off, I kept it. It didn't seem right to let someone else take over the place. It's where I keep the collection." Eugene kept his speech in a fast-paced ramble, making it more difficult to insert questions.

Iris tried to interrupt him politely. "I am sorry, I don't understand."

"It has a lovely little apartment above it. It's at your disposal. You can stay there while you work during the week. That way, you can avoid that massive commute by train every day. It will make your boss happy to save money on travel vouchers." Eugene intentionally cut her off by speaking to Julie, who had arrived. *It is so much more fun to keep the young people guessing.*

Iris's eyes had gone wide even as she tried hard to hold onto her disciplined smile.

Oh man, this is going to be fun.

"Get Miss Porterfield the old office keys. She will be staying at the apartment while she appraises things and goes over the books," Eugene said evenly before he stood up from his comfortable chair.

Julie nodded. "Of course. I will make sure to also arrange a rental car for you, Miss."

Iris tried to protest. "Mr. Bartley, I was not sent here to appraise the assets; only to give you the contract and go over the royalties and investments. That can all be done remotely. There is no need for me . . ."

"Nonsense, what's the point of me hiring a whole other person to look over my physical assets? I need someone I can trust, and I have it on good authority that you are a fan of mine." Eugene grinned as he saw the flash of embarrassment on her face. She looked down at her folded hands, and he saw the blush creep up her neck. *Aww, look at her all pink cheeked. Leroy would have had a great time teasing her.*

Iris shook her head slightly.

"I am terribly sorry; it is very unprofessional of me. I, of course, have read your novels, sir," she said down at her hands, embarrassment flooding her system. She wanted to look up and tell him how much she loved his mysteries, how she always got excited and scared. The words clogged her throat. Her head bobbed up and down in an affirming nod. She hated the emotional quicksand she was standing on. She counted in her mind and did her best to keep her cheeks from burning. *Come on, Iris, get it together . . .*

He came to her rescue. "I wouldn't want someone that didn't understand trying to tell me what my collection is worth. I am glad they sent you, Miss Porterfield. I trust you will take good care of my life's work." His tone was gentle and kind. Iris smiled and managed to suppress her embarrassment. He continued smoothly giving her time to recover. "Julie will get the keys. I will make sure all the paperwork is in order. I need you to get started right away." He took a book off a stack to the left of his chair. "Be careful on your way; the rain is quite severe today." He set the aging paperback gently on top of her briefcase as he picked up the folder full of papers that she wanted him to sign. He gave her a conspiratorial smile as he left the room.

Iris watched him leave, not exactly sure how she had so thoroughly lost control of the meeting. She picked up the paperback novel he had left. She inhaled sharply in surprise.

It can't be . . . But it was. It was an original printing of his very first detective novel. Titled simply *Mahoney*. It was the one that had launched his writing career. She carefully opened the faded cover. In scrawling but steady cursive, it read:

To Iris Porterfield,
Good Luck with your search.
Your friend,
Eugene Bartley

A smile returned to Iris's face as she carefully inspected the older novel. Iris could hear Julie returning, and she set the book inside her briefcase before closing it quickly.

Julie gave a professional smile. "Here are the keys to the

building. The apartment has been maintained and kept clean. There are furnishings but no groceries."

Iris slowly reached out and took the keys. *Maybe taking some time away from home would be best right now. I don't want to see Brenden. I am not ready to tell Mom or argue with Dad.* Throwing herself into work was probably the best way to deal with a broken heart anyway. She smiled up at Julie.

"Thank you, that's not a problem."

Before Iris could process what all had happened, she was back in the silver car and on her way to Mr. Bartley's old office building. The afternoon sun still had not broken through the clouds, but she barely noticed. Her mind was buzzing with the work she had to do. She spent most of the ride emailing with her boss to finalize the agreements.

The last leg of the trip she spent on the phone with Vanessa.

"Ok, so let me see if I have this straight. You went to surprise your boyfriend for lunch. You overhear him on the phone with someone and realize he has been using you to get to your family's wealth and connections. But instead of confronting him and kicking him in the balls like he deserves, you run off and hop a train to go do some big appraising assignment?"

Iris made a sour face as her friend did what she does best: cut through the bullshit.

"I suppose that is one way to look at it," Iris grumbled into the phone. "Some people aren't good with confrontation. If I had faced him right then, I would have broken down in tears. I refuse to let that bastard know how much he hurt me. And my boss did need my help."

These kinds of audits can take weeks. I can't leave Bogart with Vanessa for that long.

Vanessa was quiet for a moment before she sighed. "FINE . . . We will do it your way. I will stop by your place and get your clothes. Your grumpy cat and I will head out tonight or tomorrow. I have a photo shoot today, so I will go after that. In exchange for this incredibly large favor, you are going to pose for me . . . Deal?"

Iris made another face but was relieved. "Deal. Thank you, Vanessa."

"Of course. Ok, I have to go. Love you. See you soon." Vanessa's voice already sounded hurried and on the go.

Iris smiled as she felt lighter than she had in a long time.

The driver headed to the center of the city. The area had shifted over time, becoming more of a historical district. Most of the neighborhood had been demolished and rebuilt. Some sections had been restored and embellished. They were now caricatures of the structures they used to be.

The building on the corner of 34th and Main had been brought up to code, but all the old architecture was still in place. It was designed in the Moderne style. Three stories were covered in smooth concrete, gracefully curving around corners. Large bay windows were filled with lovely, frosted glass and edged in stainless steel. Sleek and streamlined, it mixed the grandeur of the Art Deco curves without all the frills and designs.

This time, the driver didn't abandon Iris at the door; he waited as she got the keys working. He set her bags inside the small front room. Once inside, he waited patiently for his tip before returning to the car.

Iris didn't see him pause at the vehicle to watch the front door close and lock, or the lights come on inside the building farther up. She did hear the motor as he drove away.

Iris's initial search of the building led her to discover two rooms full of storage boxes and glass cases stuffed with display items. *That must be from the museum days.* She smiled a bit. *That will be fun to look through later.* She continued her tour and eventually found the stairs that led up to the apartment.

The open-concept studio was cozy and clean, as promised. It had lovely hardwood floors and a small room with a nicely sized bed. There were no overhead lights inside; everything was lit by lamps. Even with all the lights on, it still had a dim but romantic quality.

Iris sighed and shook her head, looking around.

"How did you get yourself into this, Iris?" she whispered to the room. Her phone vibrated. Iris jumped; she had forgotten she turned it back on after she had been speaking with Vanessa. She looked down at the number and grimaced. *Dad . . .*

She took a big sigh and answered.

"Hello, Dad. Why are you calling me? I left you a message saying I was unavailable right now." Her voice sounded soft in the dim room.

"Iris, tell me where you are. I will come and get you." Ethan Porterfield's voice came firmly over the line. Iris hadn't returned his call or gone to lunch with clients like she was supposed to. She could hear his frustration. He only ever used that tone when something didn't go his way. She felt a smile tug at her lips. She knew he didn't like not being in control.

Iris straightened her shoulders and leaned against the counter.

"I'm not in the city. I appreciate the offer; however, I won't be returning for a while," she answered in a coldly polite rebuff. She took a seat on the stool by the counter. She held her phone in one hand and used the other to remove her shoes. She closed her eyes as she massaged her toes. She was getting better at these moments with him. His huffing, puffing, and disapproving had been so scary as a teen. Iris was proud of herself.

"This is ridiculous, Iris. You understand the situation: the merger is speeding up. There are meetings, luncheons, and parties you are expected to attend." His words came out short and clipped as the cold anger seeped into his voice.

"I am terribly sorry for any inconvenience my absence may cause. I am unfortunately detained with my own work obligations. I am afraid I won't have time to attend the *family* functions. I am certain you will be able to carry on without me, *Ethan*." Iris used his first name instead of calling him dad while she maintained a perky but polite, professional tone with icy venom underneath. She knew that would make it perfectly clear how she was feeling about the subject. *I should win an Oscar for that voice.*

She could practically hear his teeth grind. She was honestly surprised he was still on the phone. He would normally have hung up by now. At least, that was what happened the last time she had a fight with her parents.

"Iris, cut the shit."

Her eyes widened in surprise at his cursing. *This is more than anger; something must be wrong.* It gave Iris a moment's worry. She was mad at him, but she still loved him. *Why is he so desperate? The merger is going to happen one way or the other . . .* She groaned inwardly, and she kicked herself for being too soft as she eased her tone.

She leaned on the counter and took a moment to breathe. The anger was still in her voice, but she spoke in a more natural cadence.

"Alright, Father, I will if you tell me what this is really about. I am on assignment right now. I have a big client and being given a great opportunity. I am needed here; you don't need me to attend any of those functions. Why are you so insistent . . ." Iris's voice trailed off as a dark thought crept into her mind.

"Iris, this is important." Her father's voice came over the line. Iris knew the tone. It was the same one he had used since she was a child. To get her to finish homework, do chores, whenever he needed her to do something she didn't want to. "It's not just me: your mother misses you. Whatever happened, we will work it out. I am sure they could find someone else to cover for you at Brownstone. Come home." His voice was downright warm.

Her fists clenched and she felt her face tighten into a frown. *Was he on the other end of that phone call? Did he know? Has he known what Brenden has been doing this whole time? Did he put Brenden up to it?*

"Actually, no they can't. I was specifically requested by the client. They won't accept anyone else. When I am done, I will come home and we can talk. If you need me to look over the paperwork on the merger, let me know. Though we both know that isn't why you want me to get involved." Her tone was clipped, and her voice hard. "I have neither the interest nor the time to play these games. Good night, Father."

There was a heavy sigh on the other end of the phone. "Good night, Iris, I will call again." Then silence as the call ended.

Iris set down her phone and looked around the dark room. It was sparsely furnished but functional, with every-thing a person might need. The dim light helped her feel less exposed, and the space was free of clutter. It felt snug and safe. It reminded her of hiding under the table or in an empty closet.

She stood by the window and placed a hand on the glass. It was cool to the touch. The windows looked out at the gloom of 34th Street. Rain distorted the bright, garish neon lights as it ran over the outside of the glass. Pockets of bright rainbow colors spotted the slick black sidewalks.

In stocking-covered feet, she walked across the floor and turned on the old radiator heater. She rubbed her arms, trying to warm up from the chill in the air.

"Maybe a hideout is exactly what I need."

She smiled as she headed to the bedroom.

Chapter Two

HEAVY RAIN DISTORTED the images through the window overlooking 34th Street. The demonic smile of the neon sign across the street was stretched and pulled at strange angles. The glow of street lamps reflected in the pools on the concrete, creating little blue dots across the black landscape. From his seat by the cracked window, Leroy watched as specters moved through the night. A translucent bus paused to drop off and pick up poor souls forced to trudge through the storm.

He took the last pull from his cigarette and snuffed the glowing blue ember out in the ashtray. He pulled the window closed with a snap. He paused as he caught a shadowed reflection in the glass. A pretty face looking a bit sad. A faint outline of a delicate woman's hand appeared on the glass. He stood in the warm spot of air for a moment before he blinked, and she was gone. He looked around and scratched the back of his neck.

"That's odd." He shrugged as he went back to the breakfast table. He sat and picked up his coffee cup. Leaning back, he closed his eyes as he enjoyed the rich smell and flavor, tasting the memory of the many coffees he had before. He knew the steaming brew in his mug was made of the same energy as the cigarette he had just smoked. With the other hand, he picked up his copy of the *Heralds' Herald*. He skimmed the headlines, trying to relax, when the harsh clanging of the phone shattered his moment.

Setting down the paper, he rose and headed to the phone.

"What's up, Frankie?" He tried not to sound as annoyed as he felt.

"Sorry, Mahoney, there is a Warden here. Says he has to talk to you. Says if you don't come down, he'll come up." Frankie sounded rattled, but then he always sounded that way.

Leroy frowned as he considered what Jack could want. It had to be something official for him to show up here. Their meetings were usually more clandestine.

The Spirit Wardens were a special breed. They were never human, or ever living. They were the entities that guarded the dead, and they didn't exactly approve of Leroy's business.

Leroy had met the jackal Warden shortly after opening shop and Leroy started helping the in-betweeners with their tethers. Jack was the most tolerant and tolerable of the Wardens, and they were nearly friendly. At least, as friendly as a Warden and a dead detective could get.

"Don't worry about it, Frankie. Send them on up," he said brightly as if he always had Wardens up to his flat.

Leroy didn't bother saying goodbye as he hung up. He quickly finished putting on his coat and fixed his tie. He checked himself in the mirror and then leaned casually against the counter with his paper and coffee in hand.

It was important to give the right impression. Reputation was everything in this business, after all.

"Hello there, Jack," he said without looking up from the paper.

The Wardens came in all sorts of shapes and sizes, and Jack was a towering seven-foot humanoid with a dark jackal head. Leroy figured it was some remnant of the Egyptian days. His ears perked up slightly, and the glowing yellow eyes flashed before they narrowed. He didn't exactly step, he just moved. In a blink, he was inches from Leroy's face. Leroy jerked back in surprise, and his mug fell to the floor as Jack yanked him off his feet and held him in the air by his throat.

"Hey, get your paws off me. What gives!" Leroy struggled, lifting his fist to punch Jack in the snout, when another voice came from the door.

"I wouldn't fight if I were you, Leroy. Jackal doesn't like you."

Ah, I see what's happening. Jack's putting on a show for the boss.

The Warden by the door was the one Leroy dubbed Goldie. He was shaped as a lithe man with flowing locks of golden curls around his head. "He would enjoy ripping you to pieces."

Leroy knew Goldie would be the one to enjoy that.

"No fight here, just worried I broke my mug is all." Leroy gave a smirk as he held his hand up. "Isn't there a rule about Wardens ripping souls?"

Jackal snarled, his muzzle right up to Leroy's face, his fangs pearlescent as they flashed. Leroy felt a sting as Jack left a mark on his cheek. Before Leroy could complain, he was flung against a wall.

He groaned and slowly got to his feet with a pained chuckle.

"So, is there a reason you stopped by, or did you just want to make kissy face?" Leroy dusted his jacket off and straightened his tie.

Goldie smiled and picked up the mug from the ground,

setting it neatly on the counter. Jackal, on the other hand, began to systematically search the room. His nose twitched and snuffled as he flashed around the room, knocking over tables and shelves. He dumped out cupboards and closets. Leroy kept a cocky smile in place as he kept his anger in check.

"You have a client. Nelson Blakely," Goldie said, leaning casually against the counter.

It wasn't a question, so Leroy didn't answer. He picked up his mug, and the coffee steamed out of it again as he waited to see if Goldie would continue. When he didn't, Leroy smirked and took another sip.

"Is that who you are looking for inside my sock drawer?" he said over his shoulder to Jackal.

Goldie's fake smile took on a less friendly edge as he whispered, "Nelson Blakely was ripped . . ."

Leroy tried not to choke on his coffee. He looked at Goldie and then at Jackal, who had finished his search. Jackal shook his head no to some unspoken question. Goldie slowly moved closer, gently lifting Leroy's tie as if to examine it. The faded blue tie suddenly felt very tight around his neck as it trapped him in place.

"He was seen with you at the docks last night," Goldie continued calmly as he slowly wrapped the tie around his hand.

Leroy winced as he felt the cold burn of the Warden pulling on his soul. It hurt, but he knew it could get so much worse. He gritted his teeth as he fought to hold his smirk in place.

"Yeah, we were taking a romantic walk . . . aaarghh."

Goldie pulled a small chunk of Leroy off, just a tiny pinch, but the agony was real. He held up the glowing blue bit of Leroy's soul to eye level, inspected it with distaste, before he let it drop to the floor.

"Fuck . . . Cool it! I was hired to help him with his tethers. His wife crossed over, and he was worried he would be forgotten. He wanted to get them cleared up so he could join her. We found one on the docks, and I left him there. We were supposed to meet up later today to look for the next one."

Leroy yanked away; Goldie let go of the tie. He didn't look pleased as he stepped back. A dismissive sneer was on his face, and he walked out. Jackal stood there, watching as Goldie left.

Leroy snatched up the piece of himself. Putting it in his mouth, he swallowed it with a sigh of relief.

Jackal swiped a hand through the air, and the room returned to its original condition.

"Jeez, Jack, were you just going to let him rip me apart a piece at a time?" Leroy said as he slumped into his chair.

"Yes. If you had anything to do with the ripping, it would be a fitting punishment." Jackal's voice was deep and resonating but calm. He took the seat across from Leroy.

"The Arbiter is not to be taken lightly, Leroy. They are looking for a reason to be rid of you. They don't like the loopholes and grey areas you represent. You are proof that the system isn't perfect. They don't like that you help the souls pass over. They think it is unnatural, or unfair." He shrugged as he leaned forward to take one of the smokes out of Leroy's pack.

"Not my fault I am stuck here; besides, how is any of this shit fair," Leroy said.

Jackal lit the smoke with a blue flame and gave a strange canine-like smile. "I never said I agree with them. I am pleased when you help those that need to pass. Everyone should be able to pass through to the other side."

Leroy smirked a bit as he sat up, collecting himself. "Yeah, I know. I will see what I can find out about Nelson and pass along what we were working on. Speaking of work: I need to get to the office. I have a new client arriving soon. So, make tracks. I don't need your mug sending her packing."

Jackal nodded and rose, taking the cigarette with him.

"Be careful, Leroy," he said with a one-handed wave.

Leroy fixed his tie and smoothed his hair as he headed towards the door. "Time to go to work."

Chapter Three

THE OFFICE of the Bartley and Mahoney Investigative Agency had opened its doors in the winter of 1945. The frosted-glass doors were the entrance to a small reception area, with a little secretary desk across from several comfortable chairs and a coffee table. This was sectioned off by a single wooden door that led to the back office. Much of the office space was dedicated to this room.

Along the back wall were tall, locked metal filing cabinets. The central space was divided equally. It was the perfect setup for partners. On the left side was Bartley's desk, chair, bookshelves, and workspace. Mahoney's mirrored it on the right. The light came in on both sides from small windows. Hanging on the walls were photos and memorabilia from the war and the many adventures the two had shared overseas. Also hanging on the wall on Bartley's side were photos from his wedding, the birth of his son, as well as the awards he had earned from his writing career.

On Mahoney's side, there were newspaper articles of his cases as well as articles about his unusual unsolved murder, and there was a large glass display cabinet with personal effects. Mahoney's side had a bit more dust than Bartley's. Someone came through and maintained the space, though it was clear the office had not been used in a long time.

Bartley's desk had an old-fashioned typewriter, a rotary phone, and other items meant to make it look like an old-timey novelist's desk. However, Mahoney's desk had been left very much like the original. No upgrades in lighting or equipment.

When Iris came down the next morning, the office was as chilly as the apartment upstairs. Iris wore jeans and a T-shirt today but had put on a large, oversized cardigan sweater to keep off the chill. She walked over and looked at the items set on the desk. There was a newspaper that had yellowed with time. She was surprised it wasn't better taken care of. A thick grime had started to coat the oak because it had only been lightly dusted.

At one point, there had been some thoughts of turning this place into a kind of museum. There was quite a loyal fan base for Detective Mahoney. The books were profitable and had launched Bartley's career. His other book series were far more lucrative, but this was where it had all begun. She didn't really see any potential as a museum, however.

Iris spent most of the morning setting up her workstation. She opted to use Mahoney's desk because it was far less cluttered than Bartley's and would involve less moving. Bartley's area had been crammed with his life, whereas Mahoney's had been left undisturbed.

Iris spent an hour clearing out dust and cobwebs. The rain had finally ended so she opened the windows and let the fresh air in. Once the grime was cleared off the desk, she neatly stacked the papers she found there and began moving objects to make room for her things. Under the calendar placemat, she was rather surprised to find an old silver coin. It was a one-dollar coin minted the year WWII ended. She set it to the side with a small stack of handwritten notes. They seemed like random scribbling, grocery lists or some such. She didn't throw them away since she assumed they were kept for sentimental reasons.

She set up her phone, chargers, laptop, and writing utensils. There was no wi-fi in the building, so she set up her mobile hotspot. The sunshine set the office aglow and the cool fresh breeze blew in. Iris smiled with satisfaction, and she enjoyed having the quiet space all to herself.

Now that she was set up, she got started. She worked through her emails for an hour or so. She talked to her boss and began organizing the documents he had forwarded. She ordered lunch in and tried to make sense of the chaotic ledgers.

It was at lunch when she started tackling the file cabinets, trying to find out what all was here and cataloging things as she went. Most of the cabinets were filled with old paperwork. However, that was only on Bartley's side. Mahoney's side was locked. Iris went to the desk to look for a key, only to find that it, too, was locked.

Iris frowned and considered what to do for a moment. Digging through her pockets, she found and pulled out the keys they had sent her with. She flipped through them and found no desk keys, but there was one labeled "storage." She got to her feet and headed to find the storage room. It turned out to be the basement.

Once she got the light on, she headed down the staircase. Inside was a large room filled with boxes. She groaned. "And this is why I prefer the paperwork." She sighed sadly, grabbed the first box, and started back up the stairs. After lugging the box all the way up the stairs, she set it down in the center of the room. Huffing a puffing, she groaned and arched her back.

"Come on, Iris, it's not that bad. Go get another one.

Bring them up a couple at a time," she whispered and headed back down the stairs. She managed to convince herself that four boxes were enough to work on for the rest of the afternoon. After all, it wasn't like she was in a hurry. She was careful to ignore any further calls from her father.

Iris opened the first box with care. She diligently removed each item, then photographed, tagged, and cataloged them. It was a slow process at the start, but it helped ensure a more accurate end. Iris didn't mind; she liked the even pace of perfection. She barely noticed the setting sun.

Chapter Four

LEROY WAS SITTING at his desk when a strange feeling came across him. He felt a flash of heat. He took a moment and looked around his office. He was alone, but he knew his client was coming. Seeing nothing unusual to explain the warmth, he leaned back in his chair and looked out the window.

He thought over the morning's events. It wasn't just that Nelson couldn't pay his tab, but that he was ripped so close to passing over. It didn't sit right with Leroy, so he considered what to do. Despite his grim thoughts, the unusual warmth at his desk filled him, causing a sigh to escape. His office seemed brighter. He didn't know what caused it, but the atmosphere was almost perky. He smiled as he drummed his fingers along his desk.

His smile grew when there was finally a knock on his door.

"Come in," he called, trying to look busy at his desk.

The door opened slowly, and he looked up as Jason walked in. Jason had been a young man in his early twenties when he passed over. He helped Leroy find clients on occasion. Jason had said he found a young lady who needed help.

What Leroy didn't expect was how young.

A little girl was following in quietly behind him. Jason smiled and motioned for her to have a seat.

"Hey, Mr. Mahoney. This is Lucy. She was nervous about meeting you, but she is eager to get a move on with crossing to the other side."

Leroy raised an eyebrow but gave her a gentle smile.

"Hey there, Sweetheart. How are you doing?"

She sat in the chair and fidgeted with the bottom of her dress as she looked at her shoes.

"I'm ok," she whispered finally. "I miss my mamma."

Leroy nodded thoughtfully. "Yeah, I bet you do. It's always hard to leave people behind, huh?"

The little girl shook her head. "No . . . She left me behind. My mamma died in a car accident . . . She is waiting for me."

Leroy had a twist in his gut as he cleared his throat. "Oh, I see. When did this happen?" He tried to make sure he was still speaking in a pleasant voice.

The little girl peeked up at him and looked back down. "When I was five. I am nine now. I am a big girl, but I must have gotten lost on my way to heaven."

Leroy's smile turned a little sad, but he nodded. "Yeah, Sweetheart. Just a little bit longer. But we will get you there. See, sometimes what happens is we try to take things with us when we die. Ideas, feelings, hopes, things like that. They become rooted in the living world and tie us there."

The little girl looked confused. "What do you mean?" She frowned and looked at Jason for a moment. "Does that mean I am stuck here?" There was an edge of panic in her voice.

Leroy winced and shook his head. "No, Honey. Don't

worry, we will get you out of here. But first, we need to figure out why you didn't cross over immediately."

Lucy sighed and tried to not look scared. "Ok, how do we do that, Mr. Mahoney?" she whispered softly and looked at him with big dark eyes.

Leroy considered it for a moment. "I will help you find out what's kept you tied to the land of the living so you can head to Mom, ok?"

She nodded eagerly now and sat a little more forward. "Oh . . . How do we do that?" She repeated her question in that way all small children do.

Leroy smiled and looked at Jason as he crossed his hands over the desk. "Well, I need you to think very carefully. Is there something you are missing? Something you had when you were alive. Something super important to just you?"

The little girl sat very straight as she gave it serious thought. Her brow furrowed as her little hand touched her neck.

"My locket. I am missing my locket. It had pictures of my mamma and daddy and me." She searched her pockets and gasped a bit.

He smiled brightly at her and snapped his fingers.

"See? Easy peasy. We will find your locket and see if we can't send you on to your mother." He wrote down some notes and stood up.

"Good work, Jason. How much do I owe you?" Leroy looked over to the young man, who was just leaning against the doorjamb. Jason waved a hand. "On the house. I had a kid sister once upon a time. Kid was walking around, asking people if they knew how she got to heaven . . ." He held his thumb and pointer finger a tiny distance from each other. "She came this close to being turned into some-one's artifact. She really needs your help." Jason gave a little smile at Leroy. "Let me know if you need anything else. I have some errands to run, but I will be back by later."

Leroy opened a draw in his desk and slipped a few glowing blue bullets into the gun he kept in his shoulder holster. He rounded the desk and gathered odds and ends off his bookshelf: a wooden spool with a single piece of thread, a broken watch, a matchstick box, and similar bits. They slipped easily into the magic pocket tucked inside of his coat. Some of the items he gathered still held their old power, others had long since lost the glow they possessed. *You never knew what you could use on a case.*

Years stuck in between the realm of the living and the beyond had forced Leroy to learn a few things. He had far greater control of his spirit power than most. He knew how tempting a fresh bright soul like Lucy would be to those stuck in the in-between.

I will need to be careful.

"Alright, Kid, let's get a move on. No time like the present, right?"

The little girl smiled at him and took his hand. He put on his hat as he walked her out the door. She was as bright and shiny as a newly minted penny. The new souls like her still had a glow around them. Some called it the light of life. The longer they remained in the in-between, the dimmer the light became. Eventually, it would go out altogether.

It was hard to say why the glow faded. Some thought it had to do with understanding that they were dead or losing connection to their previous life. He had one client that theorized it had to do with whether someone believed you were still alive. The Wardens just said it had to do with losing your sense of self. It showed how close you were to becoming a Shade.

As they walked towards the door, the little girl stopped. She pulled on his hand as her eyes tracked something he couldn't see. She watched it pass and move back towards his desk. She smiled a bit and tilted her head as she watched whatever it was. Leroy frowned as he looked around his office. He knew something was different, but he couldn't quite see it.

"What is it, Kid? What do you see?" he asked. He knew those who had just recently passed could see better through the veil than someone who had been dead a while.

The little girl pointed excitedly. "It's a pretty lady unpacking. She is singing with the radio. My mamma loved that song . . . Oh, and she ordered pizza." She beamed up at Leroy. "Can we get pizza?"

Leroy looked at the empty space on the floor and considered it for a moment. It had been a long time since there had been any activity in the office. He pushed the thought from his mind. There wasn't anything he could do about it anyway.

"Yeah, sure, Kid. Let's go." He held the door open for her and locked it behind himself.

Lucy walked down the street, holding tight to Leroy's hand. The many denizens of the city passed through the arteries and pathways, scuttling and scurrying in flashes and blurs. Others moved in sluggish shuffles. Entities that were never human flitted around or skulked in shadows. Passing a familiar corner, Leroy slowed down near the entry to a dark alley. There, sitting against the corner, was a hunched figure. It was curled in on itself, a deep shadow of grey and misery.

He crouched down to look for the face lost in the haze of smoke.

"Hey, are you still in there, Jeff?" he whispered to it

quietly, looking around as he waited. Lucy cringed back in fear, hiding behind Leroy's long jacket.

"Mahoney?" a voice whispered, sounding like a rusted hinge opening. Lucy curled further into Leroy, peeking around the edge of the coat.

"That's right, Jeff. It's your pal Mahoney. I told you to stop drinking that stuff. It makes you forget . . . If you forget much more, there won't be any of you left."

Through the grey a face began to form. A face as thin as old paper peered up at him. The smile that came caused crinkles in the flimsy covering as he slowly started to return to the shape of himself.

"That's right . . . I used to be Jeff. That's who I was . . ." A hand formed up out of the darkness around him, rubbing his head that started to take shape.

"I remember now. I was a man once." He looked around, dazed and confused. "Or was a man, me?"

Leroy sighed and grabbed ahold of the hand. With a heavy tug, he pulled Jeff out of the clinging muddy smoke of forgetfulness. Jeff stood on legs as they appeared out of the miasma that he had been slowly dissolving into. Once he was again firmly standing, Leroy pulled a small shining coin out of his pocket and pressed it into the center of Jeff's chest. It sank into the darkness there, and after a moment, the deep shadow lightened. Jeff became more solid and alert.

"Hey . . . Leroy, long time, no see. How are you doing, man?" He smiled and looked more of himself until he was almost solid.

Lucy didn't make a sound, hoping the strange smoke man didn't see her.

Leroy continued the conversation as if nothing unusual was happening. "Hey, Jeff. No complaints. You should get off the streets, man. Maybe head down to see the Reverend."

Jeff nodded and rubbed his neck. "Yeah, maybe I should. Do you think they will have soup?"

Leroy nodded and gave him a little push. "Yeah, you know it. See you later, Jeff."

"Bye, Mahoney . . . You're good people," Jeff said as he stumbled down the road. Leroy watched him go for a moment before turning away. The little girl watched the man as he left and took ahold of Leroy's long coat.

"What's wrong with him?" she whispered as she hurried to keep up with Leroy.

Leroy took a moment to explain. "He is fading. It's what happens if you don't find your tethers and cross over. This is the in-between. We aren't meant to stay here. The Spirit Wardens say that this is the place where we shed the things that tie us to the living world so we can head to the next place."

He reached over and ruffled her head. "The tethers are things that hold us to our old lives. If we can find them or release them, we can pass on."

Lucy looked around, a little frown squinching up her brow. "So why doesn't he do that?"

Leroy sighed. "That's the problem. He has been here so long he doesn't remember what those things were, so he can't release them. He is stuck until he can remember them and let them go. If his light goes out before then, he becomes what is called a Shade. They aren't really people anymore. They are hungry shadows that are starved for light and memories."

Lucy looked down at her own glowing hand, and fear passed over her face. "Is my light going to go out?" Her voice traveled up to Leroy in a whisper.

"Nah, Kid. You are brand new; your light is nice and bright. You have a long time before you have to worry about something like that."

She sighed with relief before she studied Leroy's light. It was different from others; it wasn't so much that he was bright, more that he was just in vivid color. His tie was a pretty sky blue that matched his eyes. His hair was a dark brown and curled nicely. His coat was a light brown color. *It's like he was colored-in with better markers than everything around him.*

"What was the thing with the shiny coin?" she asked as they headed into a diner. Leroy smiled at someone inside, giving a wave as they took seats at a booth.

"You saw how he was sort of turning into mist, right?" he asked as he pulled out a menu. She nodded as she also reached out and took one.

"Well, he was losing himself, so I just reminded him who he was. The coin is called drasis. It's what we use as money here. It comes from the energy that fuels things here. Including us. It can take any shape, really. Like for instance, the pizza we are about to order. It's made of drasis. It will give us energy and help our lights stay bright."

She made a face at him as she tried to think of something that didn't sound stupid. "So, it was a magic coin that made him better?"

Leroy grinned and gave a little laugh. "Yeah, Kid, it was a magic coin that made him better. You ready for some pizza?"

She smiled, nodding eagerly. "Yes, please."

Leroy motioned to the waitress, who came over with a smile.

"Hey there, Sugar . . . You two ready?" She was an older lady with a sweet southern accent.

"Two slices and two pops, please," he asked politely, giving her a wink.

"Sure thing, Honey. Coming right up," she said with a smile, then she headed back behind the counter.

After a moment she returned with two slices of steaming pizza and glasses of fizzy soda. They looked appetizing, but there was no smell. Leroy missed the smell of pizza, a woman's perfume, heck, even the smell of stinky alleys. He knew the reason he couldn't smell it was he had never paid much attention to those kinds of things in his life. Some days he wished he had spent more time paying attention to that sense.

But he kept his thoughts to himself as he took a bite. He could feel the energy, and his mind filled in the flavor of his favorite pizza. It didn't really need to be chewed. But it was easier for newcomers to go through the motions. It took a certain amount of power to be able to transfer drasis without a ritual of some kind.

The little girl seemed to enjoy the pizza and soda. She perked up and chatted happily in the booth across from him. That was good. She would need the energy if they were going to be able to find her tether.

He kept a weather eye out for Shades or artificers. There were plenty of dangers here in the in-between. And they were all hungry. The sooner she crossed through the better. For now, he would make sure she was safe, and when she did go, she would go as gently as possible. *It is really all I can do for her here in the end. Some jobs are harder than others.* It seemed to Leroy the harder the job, the more important it was to get done.

"Hey, Mr. Mahoney?"

She broke into his thoughts, bringing back his attention to her face. She was looking up at him all hopeful and excited.

"Yeah, Kid?" he said, caught off guard a little.

"Can we have ice cream sundaes? Please?" She gave him a big-eyed pleading look.

He smiled. *I may be hard-boiled, but I am no match for that look.*

"Ya know what . . . sundaes sound perfect," he responded. "In fact, let's get banana splits." He motioned the waitress back over. "Might as well live a little."

Chapter Five

Iris let out a puff of exhausted air as she let herself fall backwards to lie flat on the floor. She groaned as she stretched out the cramps in her back. Time ticked by slowly as she focused inwardly on her breathing. Moving through her favorite yoga poses, she let her muscles relax and her spine elongate. She sighed as her weight shifted and her back popped into place. With a contented sound, she put her hands on her curved belly and opened her eyes again.

It was much later in the afternoon than she had realized. She took a moment to climb to her feet and check her phone. There were several messages from both of her parents.

She groaned and carried her phone with her as she got her coffee cup and headed upstairs to the only working coffee pot. With resignation, she pressed the play-all icon.

"Hello, my darling! It's your mother." Iris rolled her eyes as she filled the pot with water. Her mother's voice over the phone took up as much space as her presence did. It was loud and vivacious, and the background noise of activity told Iris she called while she was out of the house.

"I know you are busy, but you simply cannot miss brunch this Sunday."

Iris mouthed the words even as they came out of the phone.

"Oh, yes I can. Just watch me," she answered the disembodied voice.

Her mother's voice continued as Iris put the water into the coffee machine and pulled out her coffee grounds.

"Mrs. Cartwright will notice you are missing, and that will make you a target. I know you are upset with . . . him; and that is the exact reason you must not run away." Her mother's tone didn't shift from its brisk, cheery demeanor, but Iris could hear the steel underneath. She wasn't sure how her mother had found out. Or if they had simply guessed.

Iris didn't mock or reply. Even so far away, her emotions were raw, and she flinched. She scooped the grounds into the filter before closing the top and pushing the brew button.

Her mother's tone lowered and it filled with a cold menace. Iris shivered even though she knew it wasn't directed at her.

"You can lick your wounds later, Iris. Now is the time for revenge or retaliation. I have told you time and time again: never show them weakness. They are sharks, my Lovely, and they will eat you alive if they can. Trust me on this, Sweetie. We will make him pay, I promise, Baby. I love you. Call me." The last few words were back to a more maternal tone, though Iris knew an order when she heard one.

Iris blinked back tears. She knew her parents loved her, but their Machiavellian personalities made sincerity and empathy nearly impossible for them to express.

The next message began to play as Iris collected herself.

"Iris, it's Vanessa. I have your cat. I will bring him as soon as I can. I saw your father yesterday. He looked about ready to implode. Anyway, your fluffy boyfriend is here with me and is grumpy as ever. Remember, I am always on your side so call me if you need to."

Iris smiled softly, glad to know they were on their way.

The next message started to play.

"Iris, I have sent you several documents. I want you to go through them and tell me what you find . . . I know you are upset . . ." Iris perked up as she heard the hesitation in her father's voice. She knew her behavior had hurt him. She hated disappointing him.

"I will make sure they understand you are working. It will help if you take care of this paperwork from where you are. Maybe make a conference call." She felt a smile spread across her face. Her father was a hard man to understand, but she knew he loved her.

"Work hard, and remember . . ." His strong voice wavered for a moment before he cleared it. "I love you . . ." There was a long moment of silence before he said briskly, "And call your mother before she murders me."

Tears threaten to spill out from behind her glasses. *They are trying to support me as best they can.* She rinsed her mug as she waited for the pot to finish brewing.

"Iris . . ." His soft, smooth voice came out over the phone.

Her face lost its color and her breathing kicked up. She looked around at the sound of Brenden's voice. For a brief second, she thought he was in the room. She stepped towards the phone, pain lancing through her heart.

The way he said her name, it had always seemed different . . . special. It had made her smile, but now it just hurt.

"Iris . . . Why aren't you answering my calls? This isn't like you. Your father says you were called away on business." His voice was full of sweetness and had a gentle rhythm to it. It used to sooth her nerves and make her feel comfortable. Now it made her feel like she was being lied to.

"I know something is going on, Iris. What is it? Did you get in a fight with your mother again? Just talk to me. Whatever this is about, we can work it out."

Iris barely resisted the urge to throw the phone across the room.

"Son of a bitch!" She cursed at no one in general. She paced and chewed her lip in both frustration and anger. She took a moment to calm her breathing and tried to shake out the tension. She crossed her arms and looked around the room.

No, I am not ready to confront him about this.

She stomped her foot and walked away from her phone. She refused to think about this right now. Instead, she headed to the bathroom to take a shower.

Chapter Six

Leroy took Lucy with him to a small house at the end of the street. Keeping a firm hold of Leroy's long jacket, she walked and watched the strange people pass them by. Some were horrific, others beautiful and graceful. She never knew what to expect next. At the end of this long lane was a small but pretty house. Its lawn was neatly trimmed and seemed to be full of strange and beautiful flowers. The grass wasn't green; it was a ruby color, with blue flowers peeking up like daisies. The trees were strange colors too. Little sparkles seemed to buzz around like bees. To Lucy, it looked like something out of a Dr. Seuss book.

Leroy walked up the shiny, flat black steppingstones to the door. The door was painted white, and the rest of the house was a deep-blue color. Lucy noticed that the house sat in a center of three rings, one inside the next. Each circle was connected by little paths of smaller stones.

An old, weathered woman opened the door.

"What!" she snapped as she squinted through her little owl glasses.

She wore an undecipherable mix of skirts and shawls.

Some were brightly colored, others grey and faded. She broke into a smile when Leroy came into focus. Though her cheeks were rosy, and her expression warm, her mouth was full of stained, crooked teeth. It left Lucy a bit unsettled.

"Well, come in then," she said. Not even allowing anyone to answer, she stepped back from the door. Leroy took off his hat and smiled.

"Thank you, Bea. That is very sweet." He stepped through and gently pulled Lucy along. The door shut behind them on a silent hinge.

The inside was warm and inviting, clean but cluttered. Every shelf seemed to be filled with knickknacks and odds and ends.

Lucy walked inside, her eyes wide with wonder and surprise. It looked like something out of a fairy tale. It seemed to sparkle and glow on every surface. As she turned, the old woman waved a small twig and she seemed to melt away. A young woman wearing the same clothes stood in her place. She was pretty, with long blonde hair and bright green eyes. Her eyes flashed and glowed with their own light. She was whispering with Leroy. She laughed and seemed to sparkle again. Lucy knew immediately she was a fairy.

Lucy was so excited by the magic of it that she didn't notice some of the knickknacks watched her as she passed.

Leroy smiled at Beatrice and gave her a wink as she transformed.

"Hey, Beautiful, you trying to make me dizzy?" he whispered, and she giggled in response. It never hurt to flatter a pretty lady, though Leroy knew better than to fall for the charms of a Fae.

"Oh, you tease," she whispered back. "I know you didn't come here to flirt. Tell me about the shiny lost penny you have found here."

Leroy nodded and motioned for Lucy to come forward.

"This is my new client. She is missing a locket. I am hoping if I track it down, we can help her move on and get to her mom in heaven."

He held up two glowing coins. Bea raised a skeptical brow but didn't contradict him in front of the child. Instead, she smiled and nodded.

"Of course, dearest, don't you fret." She waved a hand and walked to a large desk. The old wood was somehow still alive. It grew out of the wooden floor. Little faces of strange imps and goblins were shaped in the bark. The smooth curves twisted and turned, weaving together to create a flat surface. Resting in a groove on the top sat a very large book. She walked behind the desk. As she did, the wood from the floor grew and twisted to form a spindle stool for her to sit on.

Once she was comfortably seated, she reached out to the enormous book. The leather binding creaked as she opened it, and the stiff thick paper flapped like bird's wings as she tapped her lip.

"Let's see who would be best. No . . . no . . . no . . . Oh, definitely not. It's just a lost little thing, but it would be shiny. Shall I send a Corax?" She looked at Leroy.

He groaned in response. "Oh, please no. Not a bird. Last time I used one of those, we spent all day chasing anything with a sparkle. Not to mention, I had to run to keep up. What about a bloodhound?"

Bea shook her head. "No, she is too fresh; her scent will be overwhelming. Besides, I thought the idea was to not traumatize the girl."

Leroy swore softly under his breath.

Bea returned to tapping her lip and flipping through the pages, but Leroy knew an innocent act when he saw one. He winced. He knew as well as Bea did who would be perfect for this job.

"Fine! Fine, you can stop tugging. We both know who would be perfect for this job," he said, rubbing the back of his neck.

"Well yes, but Mouse was pretty upset with you. You did break one of her favorite dreams. I am not sure she will work with you even if I called." Bea grinned with a kind of malicious glee. "I suppose I could force the issue, but you know what that will cost."

Leroy almost flinched but managed to keep his face placid. He shrugged. "Well, why don't we ask her and see what she says. If I need more than that, I will figure it out at the time."

Bea's smile turned a little sour. She waved her hand and the book snapped shut. When she stood up, the stool unwound and sunk back into the floor. She rose and went to the huge wall of bric-a-brac. Out of all the random items, she pulled a small pouch off the shelf.

She moved to the center of the floor and drew a small circle with her finger. There, she opened the pouch and pulled a pinch of glitter and dust out, pouring it into the center.

"One two three, one two three.

Little mouse, little mouse, hurry hurry, don't be late.

Scurry scurry, to and fro, hither and thither.

After and before, then and now,

I summon you to this place, at that time,

where you weren't, but are to be."

Leroy shifted so that Lucy could watch the swirl of magic and light fill the room. As the light faded, they could see again. He realized the dust was missing but the circle was empty.

Bea's smile disappeared completely. Her face turned thunderous as she glared at the circle. A whoosh filled the room accompanied by a high-pitched shout. Leroy had only a second of warning before he lurched to catch the young woman flying towards him.

She hit him with enough force that both landed hard on the wood floor.

Bea's smile returned. "Excellent. There she is. Good. I am certain you can work it out at this point." She waved a hand and returned the pouch to the shelf.

The woman stood up, dusted glitter off her person, and looked around.

"Ah, man. I was right in the middle of an adventure," she grumbled and then looked at Leroy with a scowl.

"What do you want, Roy? No, wait, don't tell me . . . Actually, no, tell me so I can kick you and tell you to go to hell." She spoke at a rapid-fire pace, her hands resting on her hips. She was small, reaching just about five feet. Her hair was a torrent of swirling blood-red curls, and her eyes flashed a strange swirl of aquamarine. It stood out against her dark-brown complexion. Swirls of glowing blue tendrils curled and moved across her skin as if being blown by some ferocious wind. She had a leather satchel over one shoulder and strange boots, but she wore a pair of jeans and a Hello Kitty T-shirt.

"Hello, Mouse. This is Lucy; she is lost and needs help."

Mouse glared at Leroy, eyes narrowed, but as she turned to Lucy, her expression changed. The wind blowing her swirls slowed to a soft breeze, warm and soothing. Her smile was friendly and charming. Lucy couldn't help but smile back.

"Hello, Little Lost Lucy. You are in luck. I specialize in

lost things. It's my job, actually. I help those lost things find their way back to their paths." Mouse's smile was firmly in place as she held out a hand to the little girl. Lucy took it without hesitation, and Mouse headed for the door. She had her hand on the knob when Bea thumped her cane on the wooden floor. Lucy noticed how the knickknacks on the shelves flinched away, cringing and huddling against the wall.

Mouse continued to smile as she put a hand over Lucy's shoulder, but she didn't turn. Leroy stood next to her and held out the two coins.

Bea held up her hand. "Not enough this time," she said, her smile turning sharp. Her features grew more angular.

"This is the agreed fee, Bea. Two coins for the call," Leroy said firmly, his smile fading quickly as he moved closer to Mouse and Lucy. "But I'll tell you what, since we are such good friends, I will throw in another coin as a tip."

Bea's body started to grow, getting bigger and bigger.

Mouse put a hand gently over Lucy's eyes and whispered, "Don't look, ok?"

Mouse turned to stand next to Leroy. "Buzzy Bea, you don't want to play this game with me." Mouse tilted her head, her own smile taking on a predatory edge. "Take the coins."

Leroy frowned; he didn't like how this was playing out. This was not how it usually went. *Today is just not going my way. What is it about today?* He didn't know, but he knew he didn't like it.

"Silly Mouse . . . I summoned you. You are bound within the constraints. You can do nothing inside my web." Bea grinned, her fangs finally starting to show. "Don't worry, I will only take a bit of her shine. She will still have plenty of time to pass over. It's been so long since I had someone so bright, so fresh." Bea's shawls and skirts shifted as her lower body expanded out into eight elongated legs, which lifted her up as she reached out her hands towards Lucy.

Mouse moved in a flash of quicksilver light, pulling a short sword out of her pocket. It glittered and sparked.

"What the hell!" Leroy jumped back from the two women. He opened his coat and scooped up Lucy inside it. He tucked her away in the magic pocket.

Bea snarled at the blade and hissed. "How dare you! I called you to this place."

"True," Mouse replied. Her grin was feral as she crouched, blade glinting and ready. The wind around her whipped, swirling the blue marks across her skin, lifting them around her form. "But you forget, She of the Web. I am a child of Eshu. We come and go as Fate decides; I only arrive where I am meant to be. You called; this is truth. I am here, this is truth. This does not mean your call is what brought me. Do not be so foolish to think your web can hold the wind."

Mouse's voice never rose above a whisper. Instead of disappearing under the sound of the growing tornado, it was carried up in a roar. The wind knocked things off shelves and blew into a frenzy. Bea hissed again and quickly backed away. The strands of spider silk that ran through everything became visible as the pile of glitter dust that came off Mouse at her arrival grew into a sandstorm.

Mouse smiled and sheathed her blade, the wind returning to her body.

"Because of your greed, your payment is forfeit. Let that be a valuable lesson to you. Do not try to take more than you are offered . . ."

"Troublesome, wretch," Bea snarled as she shrunk in size and her legs folded back into herself. Soon, she was standing there, her web in tatters and covered in a fine layer of dust. Her home was a mess of objects flung everywhere.

Mouse stepped back and waved a hand. With a whoosh, the dust and sand lifted, swirling back into the pouch that had been on the shelf. It flew into her hand. Once every grain of glittering powder was in the tiny bag, she secured it into her satchel.

"I am what I meant to be. Good and bad. I suggest you do not offend further." She reached out towards the door, and the wood pulled away from her hand, forming an opening for them to leave through. The door reformed once Leroy stumbled out after Mouse.

He stood there confused for a moment and stared at the closed door behind them. The house was the same, but all the colors seemed darker now, more sinister. He moved off the lawn onto the street and looked at Mouse.

Mouse skipped along beside him and grinned mischievously up at him.

"Impressed?"

He frowned, and after a moment of disbelief, he scowled. "Seriously? She was a network spider. You think she is going to work with me again?"

Mouse pouted and crossed her arms.

"She wanted to eat your adorable client! I told you before not to work with spiders. They can't be trusted."

Leroy grumbled as he put his hat back on his head. "And yes, it was very impressive."

Mouse beamed at the compliment, smoothing her hair.

With a flourish, Leroy removed Lucy from the magic pocket. Lucy gasped in surprise and looked around.

"What happened?" she said, her nine-year-old falsetto pinched into a worried squeak. "Where did I go?"

Leroy patted her shoulder. "It's ok now. I wanted to make sure you were safe. It's a magic pocket. My coat is like armor. It keeps me safe. And I can put things in it for safekeeping.

Not for a long time but for a little while. I hope it wasn't scary."

Lucy smiled a little. "No, it's ok. It was warm and felt like a hug."

Leroy looked away, fighting to keep his embarrassment from showing as he rubbed the back of his neck. "Come on, you two, let's get out of here." He started walking.

Lucy grabbed the edge of his coat and walked along. Mouse followed along behind with a happy little bounce in her step.

Once they were a few blocks away, Leroy stopped and looked around.

"Ok. Let's not waste time on this. Mouse, are you ready?"

He turned and jumped a bit to find Mouse standing far too close, invading his personal space.

"Oh yes, Lee . . . Roy. Mah . . . Honey." She stretched out his name, playing with the syllables. "I am ready." She grinned and wiggled her eyebrows. Leroy cleared his throat and adjusted his tie.

"Alright, then. Lucy, I need you to focus on the locket. We are going to use your connection to it, and Mouse is going to help us make sure we find the right path to it. So just focus on it," he said as he got ready.

Lucy closed her eyes and focused. Mouse did a weird chant he didn't understand and spun three times in each direction before she suddenly started walking. It appeared completely random to him, but he knew better than to ask.

"Follow my feet!" Mouse said and she didn't slow down. Leroy scooped up Lucy and followed behind Mouse as fast as he was able. They moved through the city and to the outskirts. Some places they moved like a blur, other times it was as if they were in slow motion. Several times they had to stop so that Lucy could refocus, and Mouse could adjust the course.

Finally, they arrived at a dilapidated home on the outskirts of town.

They stopped a good distance away. Mouse frowned as she looked at the building. The wood was black and grey, sagging with time. Yet somehow, it had not faded. Its presence seemed to dominate everything around it. The broken windows looked like jagged teeth, and the wreckage of the porch seemed to be a mouth gaping wide in a silent scream.

Mouse looked at Leroy and shook her head.

"It's in there. But it's not alone," she whispered.

Leroy frowned as he handed Lucy to Mouse. "Hold onto her. I will check it out. If anything happens, head to the office."

Mouse nodded, held onto Lucy, and shifted herself back. "Be careful, Leroy," she said in a serious voice.

He gave her a wink and turned toward the sleeping horror of a house. Moving in quietly, he stepped up to the window. Nothing . . . A blank oppressive emptiness stirred inside of the building as if it were breathing. He moved slowly around to the door. It hung open on one hinge.

Leroy slipped his gun out of its holster and tucked his hat on tighter.

He moved in as quietly as he could across the floorboards. He could feel the cold pulling at his skin. This wasn't an empty place; it was full of hateful things. It was a place of torture and pain. That pain tried to seep into him through his mouth and in his eyes.

He could hear in faint screaming echoes the suffering

that had come here before. The pain started to overwhelm him. He stumbled, almost falling, as he pulled himself along the wall. His coat smoldered as it tried to protect him from the miasma of sorrow and fear that filled the air.

There the locket was, in the backroom. Hidden behind a dresser was a tiny sparkle of light. He reached for it. Then he heard it. Well, he felt it, was more accurate. The vibration of rage. The blackness rose up around him. The room was full of Shades and terrors.

No, these aren't Shades. Shades are empty, these things are full. They are bursting with all the emotions left by the nightmares that had taken place within these walls.

They began to swarm him. Claws and teeth ripping and pulling at him. They tried to take him whole and bits at a time. He fired his weapon, bolts of blue energy smashing into the black. They flinched away but did not stop.

He scrambled, running for the doors as the black rose up like bubbling tar, chasing him through the hallway. He made it all the way to the door, gripping the edge as it started overwhelming him.

"Leroy!" He heard Mouse shout his name as a flash of searing pain exploded around him.

He was surrounded by sunlight. He could smell grass under his head. He could feel the heat of the sun on his cheek, the coolness of a breeze as it blew over him. He heard a soft woman's voice whisper his name. He felt content and calm as she moved over him. He could feel her reach up to pull his hat off his face. As the light blinded him, he blinked and woke up.

Mouse was on one side of him, Lucy on the other. Both

were glowing brightly, causing him to squint a bit. Eventually his eyes adjusted. He groaned as the pain returned. *It always hurts when bits of your soul get ripped off.* He looked down at himself. *At least most of me is still here.*

They were a few blocks away from the den of darkness.

"I thought I told you to make tracks," he grumbled as he sat up.

"Yeah, well, since when do I ever listen to you?" Mouse said and grinned. "Besides, Lucy is attached to you. It would make her sad if something ate you. Right, Luce?"

Lucy sniffled and threw her arms around his neck.

Leroy smiled awkwardly and patted her back. "It's alright, Kid. I am just peachy, see?"

Lucy leaned back and looked at him. "Really, really?" she whispered.

He nodded. "Yeah, right as rain. They just took me by surprise, that's all. Don't worry, now that we know where it is, we will figure out how to get it out of there."

Lucy sighed and nodded.

Hours later, Mouse and Leroy were still arguing about how to accomplish this.

"I am telling you, Roy, there is no way to remove it. I have tried everything. It's trapped inside another tether. Someone living is keeping it there. Someone living is going to have to remove it."

Leroy swore and shook his head. "How about you just cross over, walk in, and get it? You're not dead."

Mouse sighed, exasperated. "You know I wouldn't be able to walk in there, even in the living world. You have more protection from those things than I do. I have more power here than there."

"Why don't you just pop over there and grab it and pop back?" he asked, confused. "I have seen you just waltz in and out of all kinds of places. Including places without doors."

She smiled sadly. "The problem isn't the physical location. It's the stuff surrounding it. The barriers aren't just in this world, but across the veil in the living realm. I would have to fight my way through. And those aren't Fae. That is mortal pain and death."

Lucy reached up and grabbed Leroy's sleeve, pulling him down to whisper in his ear, "She got hurt when she grabbed you." She motioned to Mouse's right arm.

Leroy blinked and looked over to where Mouse was casually keeping her right arm from his view. He walked over and grabbed it. She gasped and winced.

"Damnit, Mouse," he said, forgetting what they were talking about as he began to tend her wound. It was like a bubbling burn.

She blushed and looked over at Lucy. "I told you not to tell."

Lucy frowned and looked at her toes. "Daddy always said if anyone is hurt, you should tell someone."

Mouse looked sheepish and gave her a smile. "Your dad is right. Sorry, Lucy. You're a good girl."

Mouse gasped and writhed a little as Leroy poured something from a flask over the wound. It sizzled on her skin, and she cried out, trying to wriggle free, but he held her fast. Finally, it stopped, and she whimpered as he then rubbed something else across the top, and the pain finally stopped.

When she looked, she was surprised to see the wound was gone completely.

She was marveling at the healing skin when Leroy sighed.

"I need someone from the living world," he finally said.

She looked up and frowned. "Is your old partner still alive?"

Leroy nodded. "Yeah, he is pretty old, but he has a grown grandson. Maybe we can get him to do it." He sighed and shrugged. "Let's head back to the office. I need to rest and so do the both of you."

They all nodded in agreement, and they started the trek home.

Chapter Seven

IRIS WORKED through the afternoon and into the evening, sorting out old case files as well as suitcases with old suits and personal belongings from the late Mr. Mahoney. She was waist deep in these stacks when a knock came from the front office door.

She looked up with a smile. *Oh, maybe that's, the pizza I ordered.* With the enthusiasm that came from hunger, she hurried to the front office door.

It was with that level of eager energy that she opened the door.

A well-dressed man, perhaps a year or two older than herself, was standing there, looking a bit startled by her eager arrival. Iris noticed immediately he didn't carry any food bags.

"Hello, may I help you?" she asked quietly.

A charming smile appeared on his face, flashing a dimple. He looked vaguely familiar, but she wasn't sure where from.

"Hello, Miss Porterfield. My name is Johnathan Bartley.

Mr. Bartley's grandson. I came to see if I could be of assistance."

She blinked in surprise but smiled and held out a hand. "Oh, of course. Um, thank you . . . Please come in," she said. Realizing she was blocking the door, she stepped back and held it open.

Walking in, he looked around, amused. "Wow, you really went to work, didn't you?"

A blush creeped up her neck as she looked away to regain her composure. "Yes, well, I prefer to keep busy. I have some coffee. Would you care for some, Mr. Bartley?"

He smiled and nodded. "That would be delightful. Please, call me John. Whenever someone says Mr. Bartley, I look for my grandfather."

As he took off his jacket, Iris tried not to notice his nice shoulders or pretty-boy face. *He looks like he casually leans against things while staring intensely into the distance in a magazine.* He dressed to compliment his long, lean frame. Light ash-blond hair was cut perfectly to highlight his features, and she could tell he had a manicurist.

Without meaning to, she found herself studying his shoes and pant legs. Shyness was taking root in her mouth. Swallowing hard, she tried to dislodge it while he chatted pleasantly about how he had been helping his grandfather categorize his collections.

"I don't know why he kept so much of this. It has more sentimental value. Most of this is from when he worked here."

Iris brought the coffee out. "You mean when he was writing?"

John smiled and shook his head. "Oh no. When he and Mahoney worked together. This was their office. My grandfather was a private detective back then. Eugene didn't take up writing until he decided PI work just wasn't the same without his buddy Leroy." He took the cup from her hand gently and smiled over the rim. "Thank you, Iris. Is it alright if I call you Iris?"

Returning his smile softly, she took a sip of her own coffee. "Yes, of course . . . Thank you." She winced inwardly at her own awkward words. "So, you don't think there is much value here?" she asked, trying to get back to a topic she was more comfortable with.

He shrugged. "It's valuable to him. It's his life, so yeah, it's precious. Though, I don't know why he needs to have it appraised."

Iris gave a little encouraging wave. "Oh, don't worry, it's not that uncommon. It's good for insurance policies, and he is getting older; it will help with his will and probate. That's usually the reason most people do it. But I am not aware of his thoughts on the matter."

John continued to look around at all the open boxes. "Well, whatever the reason, you have a big job. Can I help in any way?"

With a nervous chuckle and a shake of her head Iris said, "Oh no, I would love to have the help, but that's not really allowed at this stage. Not to mention, I have a whole system worked out and it would take twice as long to teach it to you than to just do it."

He gave a little chuckle before responding. "Ouch. Well, that was a quick turn down. I know us rich kids have a reputation, but I have been known to learn a few things."

Iris flushed, feeling mortified. "Oh god, no . . . I didn't mean to imply anything . . . I am sure you are very capable of handling me—it . . . I meant *it* . . . I just . . . Oh lord," she pressed, her hands against her burning cheeks.

"How about I just take you to dinner?" John said, interrupting her stuttering embarrassment, "Maybe next week?

Wednesday, pick you up at eight p.m.?" With a dashing smile, he collected his jacket.

Iris gave a little laugh. "Yes. Thank you," she said before she could think better of it.

He stopped briefly by the door to leave his card on the front table.

"Ok, see you here at eight, next Wednesday. Good night, Miss Porterfield," he said as the door clicked closed.

Iris blushed deep red, her cheeks almost on fire. *Well, you really made a complete idiot out of yourself there, Iris. But you did it. You said yes.*

The happy glow lasted for about twenty minutes as she went back to work. Slowly, her blushing calmed, and her brain began to function again.

Why would he come all this way? If he was sent to help, why hadn't anyone mentioned him? Why would he flirt so much so fast? Her inner doubts plagued her, and soon she found herself playing internet sleuth. "Hmm, well, he does work for his grandfather. But why would they hire me if the grandson can take care of his other collections? Is he the one Eugene suspects?" she asked the empty room.

Suspicions firmly rooted now, she began to sift through the mountains of paperwork and transactions. She tracked all the estate's balances and accounts. Before long, it was well into the night hours. Though it would take days to sift through the information, a pattern began to emerge. She could see the small discrepancies that accumulated over the years. The biggest red flag was the suspicious shifting of money between accounts. That was often a tactic used to hide lost amounts. If she was right, someone was slowly siphoning cash from the collection funds, little bits at a time.

Perhaps that was why he had come: to see if I found it already. Iris frowned. Disappointment filled her for a moment. *Men, they always have an angle.*

With a disappointed sigh she smoothed an unruly strand of hair out of her face. "Knock it off, Iris. He isn't worth it. Besides, it is never a good idea to date someone related to the job. And aren't you in the middle of a big messy emotional break up? This isn't a romcom," she muttered to herself as she saved her findings and sent them to her encrypted cloud. She had the pattern, but she didn't have the evidence. She would have to keep looking if she was going to be able to show any wrongdoing.

She shut down her laptop and organized her documents to take them upstairs with her. Closing up the office windows and making sure all the doors were locked, she took one last look around before she turned out the lights.

Upstairs, she showered, changed into her sweats, and climbed into the surprisingly soft bed. Cuddling down, she took up one of the many books from downstairs to read, her laptop resting next to her on the bed. The window was open enough to let in the enjoyable breeze.

Chapter Eight

Lucy sat on the swing, watching Mouse and Leroy argue back and forth like a weird tennis match. They had been trying to get her locket out of the scary house for a long time now. She didn't understand most of what they were saying.

Lucy kicked her feet back and forth to get the swing started. Once she was moving, she smiled brightly. The world was strange here. The sky never seemed to get very bright, there wasn't any wind, and the sun didn't move. Even swinging was strange. She couldn't feel the wind, but the sensation of movement was there. She found that much more interesting than the conversation of the adults.

"I am telling you, Leroy, it's not that simple. We can't just go possess a person and make them get the locket out of that house. Possession isn't easy to start with, and you know the punishments the Wardens give when they are forced." Mouse shifted to a cross-legged position on the park bench. She looked from Leroy over to where Lucy enjoyed the old swing set. The park was a mishmash of faded scenery and forgotten play equipment. Lucy was the only ghost child in the park.

Leroy sighed in frustration as he paced, his hands fiddling with the brim of his hat. "I know! But I don't know what else to do. I don't have any connections among the living. Eugene is a non-starter. He is in his nineties and shouldn't even get out of bed."

Mouse gave him an exasperated look. "That's what happens when you have been dead for more than fifty years. Honestly, it's amazing you haven't faded by now. Those novels really saved your ass."

Leroy gave a nod of agreement. "I know. I just wish he hadn't taken so much artistic license. Did you know I didn't smoke when I was alive? Now I feel like a damn chimney. I'm a detective cliché." With a disgusted sound, he put out his smoke.

Mouse laughed and nodded. "Yeah, but your fans love it. You have a strong female following." She wiggled her eyebrows.

Leroy grinned. "Yeah? It's good to know I am still popular with the ladies." He nodded and scanned the playground. He rubbed his chin as he considered the problem. "We need to find a loophole. Eugene is too old. If he finds out, he will try and get involved. His heart couldn't take that place. His grandson, John, is young and healthy, but I'm not allowed to possess him—What about a medium to try and talk to John?"

Mouse wobbled her hand back and forth. "That's hit or miss. John might not believe them or think they are scam artists. Even if he does believe, that doesn't mean he will do it."

Leroy paced back and forth as he considered that. "What

if we could make him see me? Not possess him, just haunt him?"

Mouse laughed. "Seriously? You know how hard it is to get someone who doesn't have an innate talent to see a spirit? You can haunt a location, or a person, but to do both? You have to have a serious connection."

Leroy gave Mouse a smirk. "Hard, but possible. We just need to find a way to link us, right?"

Mouse looked uncertain. "I don't like where this is going. You would need the strongest of connections to get him to see you clearly and understand you."

Leroy waved a hand. "Yeah, sure. I get him to get the locket, and then we can move on and see what other tethers we can sweep up."

Mouse frowned and stood up. "Leroy, you aren't listening. You would need the strongest of bonds . . . Like the kind made of blood or love. Something like that. And since I don't think he is going to fall in love with you, that means blood. How exactly do you expect to have your blood mingle when you have been dead for decades and you aren't supposed to hurt people?"

Leroy smiled, considered that, then snapped his fingers.

"Well, I was murdered in my office. My blood had a good long time to seep into the wooden floor. Not to mention, I was shot with my own gun. The place is full of things that are connected to me. We get him there, and one little drop of blood on the floor—boom, there we go."

Mouse raised an eyebrow and considered it. "That may be so, but how do we get him there? It's still a big stretch for the odds."

Leroy gave Mouse a cheeky, mischievous smile. "Come on, you are an expert in these kinds of things. Random acts of fate leading to major life changes, right?"

She glared at him. "That is not how it works. I don't

change peoples' fates. I don't tell the Fates what to do. I roll the dice and see what Fate decides. The Fates do as they will."

He shrugged. "Roll the bones. What's the worst that can happen?"

She groaned as she sat back down. "Were you always such a reckless gambler?"

He leaned in and gave her a charming smile. "Yo, how can I lose with such a Doll looking out for me?"

She rolled her eyes as she shoved his face away. "You aren't asking for a lucky roll. You are asking me to load the dice. You know luck hates a cheater. Even if I tried what you are asking, there is no telling how it will play out. Something might happen, or nothing could happen, or we could make the situation much worse. Are you sure it's worth it?"

Mouse's expression was grim as she stared hard at Leroy.

Leroy looked at Mouse and then at Lucy. "Have a heart, Mouse. Look at her. She is what? Nine? She barely got to live. She doesn't deserve to be stuck here."

Mouse studied Leroy with narrow eyes. "You sure it's not about the payout you would get when she crosses? All that shiny drasis she will leave behind?"

Leroy gave her a slightly angry look. "Don't be a pill, you know me better than that. She needs help, and I can help her. Sure, I get paid, but that's not—" Searing pain cut off his sentence.

Mouse's cry mixed with Lucy's scream as a figure made of red-and-orange flame snatched the little girl from the swing. Leroy lunged towards the fiery being. His hand charred in the blazing heat as he grabbed hold of Lucy's. He felt her cool fingers grip his wrist. Their eyes met before the light became blinding. He felt his hand rip apart as she was torn from his grip.

Agonized screaming filled his ears. It was too loud, but

the pain in his hand was so intense he couldn't tell them to shut up. When he was finally able to speak, he realized. *Oh . . . I was the one screaming.* It took a short eternity for Leroy to find himself. He was lying on the ground, curled into a ball around his mangled hand.

Mouse stumbled over, falling to her knees next to Leroy. Tears were in her eyes. Lucy was nowhere to be seen. Rage pushed the pain out of him, and he was able to rise.

She was taken . . . Stolen, ripped right in front of me, right out of my hands.

He roared at the sky . . . Mouse sat next to him as the Wardens arrived, late as usual.

He sat down and waited for the Spirit Wardens to approach. In a tight whisper to Mouse, he said, "Whatever the price. We are going to save her, you understand?"

Mouse looked at him with grim determination. "Yes. Don't worry, the price will not be your burden alone. I will see to it."

Iris felt a swell of panic as her eyes flew open. Her breath fogged around her face as she bolted upright in bed. The light of the bedside lamp flickered back to life as if it had gone out. She shivered in a cold sweat as she looked around the apartment.

In the dimness, the only sound she could hear was her heart pounding in her ears. She pressed hard against the wall, her knees slowly curling towards her chest. The taste of coppery panic filled her mouth as she tried to pull air through a tight throat.

Jagged shadows were cast by the little table lamp through

the suddenly cavernous room. The air was chilly and ominous in the vacant space.

"Hello?" her voice sounded small, cracked and brittle.

She swallowed hard and rubbed her arms to fight the chill. Silence responded without fanfare. As her heart slowed, she was able to hear the world outside. Rain had returned with an angry vengeance. She rose and closed the window.

Reflections of the neon lights off the wet streets looked up at her. They were the tiny glowing eyes of black spiders in the webs of the city. She frowned and looked at the night sky as it rumbled angrily. A flash of lightning crackled, illuminating the dark for a startling heartbeat.

The clouds were black waves crashing into each other. Iris quietly counted the seconds until the thunder boomed afterwards.

Closing the curtains, she took a few calming breaths. There was some relief in finding the cause of her panic. She turned off the lights.

After turning up the heater, she climbed back into bed. She pulled the covers up over her shoulders and slipped in her ear buds. Music played, pushing away the storm raging outside the window. *I hope the morning brings sunshine and warmth again.*

Chapter Nine

LEROY SAT at the picnic table next to Mouse. His hand was slowly healing as they were both carefully bathed in a replenishing drasis energy. Jackal sat down across from him as Spirit Wardens swarmed around them. In his head, Leroy replayed the moment over and over. He kept seeing the look in Lucy's eyes while their hands were ripped apart. Pain lanced through him as he unconsciously clenched his healing fist.

"Hey, calm down, would you? You are starting to crackle," Mouse whispered to him. He realized little arcs of blue energy were swirling around his body and her hair was standing on end.

He cleared his throat and nodded. He counted in his mind, trying to find some inner calm. The blue lightning subsided but settled just below his surface.

Jackal watched Leroy. After a glance at the other Wardens, he moved closer and made a show of checking his injury.

"This isn't the first time this has happened. There have been six so far." His voice was barely a whisper.

Leroy frowned as he leaned forward to look down at his hand. "Same strange light?"

"Same burning light. Same scorch marks. We know what it is."

Leroy's frown deepened as he snarled low in his throat. "Then why are you sitting here holding hands with me, Jack? Go get that asshole."

Jackal continued the show of looking over his wounds. "Spirit Wardens are not allowed to interfere with or travel to the world of the living."

It took Mouse a moment to make the connection, but Leroy was already there. The monster they had seen was a living soul. "How is that even possible?"

Jackal shrugged. "It isn't that unheard of for the living to respond or interact with the world of the dead. Some humans have a natural talent for it. In centuries past, there used to be whole religions and priests dedicated to the study of the afterlife. Books were written, secrets passed on."

Mouse gave a wane smile. "Like the book of the dead?"

Jackal nodded. "Just so. Now, I believe the term is necromancer. Though, I prefer calling it dead magic. Unfortunately, it doesn't matter; as long as it is a living person in the living world, there is little we can do."

Leroy gritted his teeth in anger. "So, they are stealing dead children? And you are just going to sit there?!" He managed to keep his voice a whisper, but he started to crackle again.

Jackal shook his head. "This is the first child that was taken. And no, I am not just sitting here. I am speaking to *you*." Obsidian eyes stared out of the dark jackal face, waiting, watching. Leroy felt the weight of Jack's gaze as his mind cleared.

Jack waited for Leroy's rage to reduce enough for him to think clearly. Jackal could see the comprehension fill Leroy's face. Jackal knew he was treading on a thin line. If it were up to him, he would hunt for his stolen souls to the edge of the world and bring them back. But rules had changed since he was transporting the dead to be judged at the scales.

Leroy looked at him, surprised, and nodded. "What can you tell me?"

Jackal smiled slowly; though with his muzzle, it was more frightening than pleasant. "I have been ordered to not tell you anything in regard to our ongoing investigations." He shifted his gaze to the Fae sitting next to Leroy. "Mouse, did you know that the Spirit Wardens are products shaped and molded out of the beliefs and devotion of the souls that pass through the in-between?"

Mouse looked very confused but gave a shake of her head. "No, I didn't know that. What does that mean?"

Jackal gave his muzzle a soft scratch. "It means that I look as I do because I am a remnant left from the old ways, where people believed Anubis was the guardian of the dead. There are those that still believe in the old gods. We shift and change as memories and beliefs change, but I am still here . . . I've learned many things about rules."

He pulled out a small scroll and handed it to Mouse. "I was very specifically ordered not to tell Leroy what I know about the investigation."

He gave a nod as he rose and walked away.

Leroy watched Jack leave. Flexing his fingers, the pain in his hand was finally gone. He got to his feet and helped Mouse up. "Let's make tracks. We need to get to my office."

Mouse nodded and they left the park.

Once inside his office, he closed the door with a snap behind them, locking and putting up wards.

"Quickly now, what does it say?" he said to Mouse as he closed the curtains.

Mouse had already opened the seal and was studying the contents.

"It's a list of the other victims and what they know about them."

With a frown and a shake of her head, she handed it over to Leroy. He sat down in his chair, read the list once quickly, and then again slowly.

"I don't get it. They seem random. Why would anyone want to take these souls? They are all different ages, men and women, different backgrounds, occupations." His frown deepened as he glared at the scroll as if the information could be intimidated into making sense.

"Maybe who they are isn't important. It can't be easy to steal souls. If it was easy, more people would do it. So maybe any soul will do," Mouse said, more to herself than him.

Leroy nodded. "Ok, so I have the ability and know how to slip through the veil and snatch a soul, but instead of capturing beautiful, powerful souls, I just grab the nearest one I can find."

Mouse follows his train of thought. "If I am grabbing at random, then why didn't I take you too? If it's about just grabbing the nearest or the most, why not take you and others? Why just one at a time?"

Leroy frowned and nodded. "Ok. So, not random. They must have something in common."

Mouse rubbed her hands over her face. "You mean, besides the fact that they're all dead?" Her tone was tired and sarcastic.

Leroy blinked as he looked at Mouse, and not because her usual perky personality was taking a dip. No, it was because the words caused a chain reaction in his brain. His subconscious made leaps as his mind tried to keep up.

"No, not dead . . . They aren't dead . . .," he muttered as he started going down the list again.

Mouse looked over at him in concern. "Umm, Roy? Are you ok? They're spirits of dead people . . . Dead is in the name."

Leroy ignored her remarks as he followed his thoughts, trying to catch up to his own idea.

"No . . . no . . . Not just dead, *murdered*!" he said as he found where he had seen it on the page. Going down the list, he saw each was the victim of foul play. He pointed it out to Mouse. "Whoever this is, is stealing the souls of murder victims."

Mouse frowned as she considered that, her blue marks swirling.

"Twice killed, twice victimized." She nodded to herself. "That will do . . . Someone is breaking the rules, hurting those that have already been robbed. Now, it's not about your case; now, it's about justice and fairness. And we need a person in the living world to help you." She stood up, her face grim. "Now, I can do it. I will roll the bones, call the Fates. But I give you this warning: even if you get what you want, that does not mean it will be as you expect or as you like. Twisting is what the Fates love to do."

Leroy nodded and took a deep breath.

"Yeah, me and the ladies have danced before. It's ok, I can take it."

Mouse stared at Leroy's determined expression. She hoped the Fates would be kinder this time around. "Alright, Leroy, let us begin."

Chapter Ten

Iris heard drums beating in the distance. No, not drums, maybe ocean waves. She looked around as she stood in a field filled with wildflowers and grass. The sky was dark and filled with stars as the sun warmed her.

She looked down and realized she was sinking. Warm mud was sticking to her feet. Making a face, she pulled her foot free and started walking. She didn't think about where she was going, just kept her feet from sinking into the hot muck. Finally, in the distance she saw a tree line. Eager to find some more stable ground, she headed to an enormous tree, its thick roots sprawling out and around, sinking down below the surface.

Once she found a root to walk across, she was able to follow it all the way to the base of the tree. She sat down on the big dry root and looked around. The sun was setting, and the sky was getting lighter as the moon came into view.

Iris watched the world shift colors as the whispering started. At first, it was the wind blowing through the branches. But soon, she was pressed against the smooth bark of the tree. She heard the words echoing as if the massive tree were hollow.

"We call out to you, we beg you. Heed us, help us. We put our trust in the Fates. This man will roll the bones, he will take his chances. He spins the wheels of destiny. I beseech the Fates to judge his cause, his merit. Help us balance the scales. Grave injustices were done. Innocents were harmed, what was lost was stolen. Allow us the chance to set things right. This is his path. Please place him upon it. So that he may walk it."

There was a crackle of lightening. The tree throbbed and shifted. It seemed to peel itself open. Iris tried to move away, but vines and tendrils of light were wound around her body. They were warm and bright, and she was completely entangled in them. She screamed and fought, as she was lifted high into the air. The beautiful faces floated in the light caused her to freeze. They brushed her cheek, and the faces came near . . .

"You need to wake up."

Iris frowned as she realized that, yes, she was sleeping. Though she had no idea why she didn't want to leave.

"Wake up . . . now!"

Iris's eyes popped open as she looked around. The room was completely dark. Even the lights on the street were out. The only thing she heard was the pounding of rain on the glass. She frowned, putting her glasses on as she looked out the window. The whole area was dark.

She tried the lights, and nothing. Looking at her phone, she saw there was no service.

"Shit, it must be a power outage."

She thought about going back to sleep but decided against it. She headed to the kitchen to get a drink. She slid on a man's flannel robe from the closet to ward off the chill. Using the light from her phone, she searched the kitchen until she found a few candles and set them up for the ambient light.

Yawning, she put the kettle over the burner. It clicked and glowing blue flames sparked to life. She reached for her tea box. Her hand was extended, the box almost in reach, when a loud heavy clunk echoed downstairs. Iris froze.

Her mind glitched. *It's my cat . . . Yeah, it's the cat . . . But Iris, you left your cat back home.*

She hugged her box of tea to her chest as she waited in the dark . . . in the silence. The silence started to bring her comfort, and she had almost convinced herself it was nothing. *Maybe a mouse.*

"Where the hell is it!" a deep voice whispered from somewhere downstairs. She clamped a hand over her mouth to keep from screaming. Her eyes wide, she looked around. She grabbed her phone, silently cursing when she saw there was still no service.

She moved to her purse and pulled out her little bottle of mace. Fear heightened every one of her senses. The smooth, cool wood floors beneath her bare feet. The sound of the storm blowing outside. The weight of the men's house robe on her shoulders.

Without thinking, she tucked the box of tea into her pocket and headed towards the door of the apartment. She pressed her ear against the crack between the door and the frame. She could hear things being moved and disturbed downstairs.

They are looking for something. But if they are thieves, wouldn't they be taking, not looking?

She was twisted by the need to know, the deep-seated

curiosity. She hated that it was true. *I will always be the first to die in a horror movie.* She took a breath to steady herself before she took ahold of the doorknob. She tried desperately to remember if the floors creaked. She kept pressed up against the wall to avoid the weak points. Years of shyly avoiding notice were paying off as she moved down the stairs. The lights were still out as she peeked around the doorframe. She saw a man with a flashlight digging through the boxes and file cabinets.

She didn't know what he could be looking for in those. He was medium height, with a mop of greasy brown hair. In the light given by the flashlight, she could see that he was wearing gloves. In the flashes from lightning, she could see that he had torn through several of the boxes. She was so intent on watching the man, she didn't notice the shadows shift behind her.

Leroy growled in frustration as he listened to the silence around them. Mouse had finished the ritual and was putting away the objects surrounding them in a circle. After a moment, he couldn't sit anymore and stood up.

"Are you sure we did it right?" he asked as he paced.

Mouse rolled her eyes. "Yes, of course I am. The ritual is complete. But Fate can take time to work. You need to be patient."

Leroy continued to prowl around the room.

"Not exactly my strong suit," he mumbled as he made another pass by the window. "How are we supposed to know if it even worked?"

Mouse smirked a bit. "What? You were expecting a big flashy light display? Some being to show up and hand you a box or something? We both know that's not how Fate works."

Leroy nodded. "Fine, so what do we do next?"

Mouse considered it for a moment. "The idea is that Fate helps us on our quest, so you proceed as if it will already succeed. I believe you wanted to form a connection to the living through the office and the objects in it. I suppose you should start there. You need to follow your tethers back to the objects and infuse them with energy. That will help them form the bridge."

Leroy nodded and started downstairs. He reached his desk and pushed his senses outward. His vision blurred a little as he felt the energy around him change. It was as if he was watching what had been happening in the space while he was away in fast-forward.

The light shifted quickly as weeks passed. People popped up cleaning or leaving things. As the past caught up with the present, it slowed down. He watched a woman come into his office. *The woman reflected in the window glass.* She sat at his desk and unpacked boxes. He recognized some of the items, but many he didn't. He watched as she moved around, worked, and headed upstairs to sleep in his bed. *I don't know how I feel about that.*

The focus came back downstairs as he watched two men slip through the front door. They moved through the darkness, searching through his belongings. Fear and anger surged as he thought about the woman sleeping upstairs. Without hesitation, Leroy pulled his fist back and swung at the man digging through the cabinet. His fist passed straight through the intruder, but it had some effect because the man flinched and knocked a book over.

The second man shushed him as he headed down into the basement.

They know she is here. Leroy panicked as he considered

what these men might do. He turned to head upstairs, but froze in his tracks as he saw her creeping down the steps.

"No . . . no . . . Go back upstairs!" he shouted at her.

She, of course, could not hear him.

"Mouse . . . What is happening? She isn't supposed to be here. She could get hurt."

Mouse was standing there but looked transparent. "You were warned. I don't control how it works. Fate has been set into motion. There is nothing I can do. You have to figure it out."

Leroy watched as Mouse began to fade. "Where are you going?"

Mouse looked around and down at her hands. "I must have done what I was meant to. I will come back when I can. Remember, Leroy, make the best of what you have got. Keep her alive, and make it work . . . You asked for a chance, and you got it. Don't waste it!" she shouted, but her voice was little more than a whisper as she disappeared.

Leroy spun back to the woman peeking around the corner at the man going through his files. He tried shouting, waving his hands and even tried pushing her.

Nothing.

He watched the second man coming up behind her. He threw punches that had no effect. He passed through the woman as he tried to get between them, and maybe some of his fear affected her because she turned at the last instant and screamed.

Her scream echoed through the house, hurting Leroy's ears.

It startled all the men. The one by the cabinets jumped nearly out of his skin; the other rushed her.

"No!" she shouted as he drew close. Her knee came up into his groin as she tried to dodge away.

"Bitch." He groaned as he managed to keep on his feet

but bent at the waist. He gripped her housecoat, pulling it off as she jerked away. The man from the cabinets came towards her, and she turned to face him.

"What are you doing, Woman! Run! Move your sticks!" Leroy shouted at her. She did not. Instead, she took an angry step forward and shouted.

"Get out!"

She then lifted what looked like a little canister towards him. A tiny stream of liquid shot out of the canister and the man screamed, grabbing his face and eyes.

"My eyes! My eyes! It burns!" He fell back, landing on his butt and a stack of cardboard boxes.

Leroy stared with wide eyes as he watched the short and curvy woman aggressively spray her assailant until the canister was empty. She then threw the can at him, hitting him in the head. The other man got to his feet and lifted her bear-hug-style.

"Stop it! Give us what we came here for, and we won't hurt you."

She kicked and squirmed in his grasp as he lifted her clean off her feet. The woman might have been short, but she was built solidly, with plenty of extra cushioning. It was no easy task to keep her up off the ground.

She looks angrier than a wet hen.

"Holy moly! You've got a tiger by the tail there, pal . . .," Leroy mumbled, some of his fear replaced by admiration for the lady.

She took a deep breath and calmed down a little. "Ok, ok. I know right where it is."

Leroy blinked in confusion and then smirked. "Sly . . ."

The man nodded and slowly set her on her feet. He looked over to his friend, who was still rolling and grabbing his face. "You ok there, man?"

"My eyes! The bitch maced me . . .," he shouted as he rolled to his knees. "I can't see . . . Oh, it hurts."

The bear-hug man tried to decide what to do. He took ahold of her arm as he moved over to help his friend. Leroy grinned as he waited to see what happened.

He was not disappointed. She let herself be dragged closer to the hurt man, which took her past several objects, one of which was a small metal statue of a cat. She grabbed it quite easily.

Leroy expected her to swing at his head and was surprised when instead, she swung the impromptu weapon full force on the side of the man's knee. The assaulted appendage buckled underneath him, leaving him in the perfect position for the shorter woman to hit him square in the face. There was shouting and flailing as the man rolled away from her, holding his broken nose. She ran to the other side of the room. With surprising accuracy, she hurled objects at the two men, screaming like a banshee.

She's got one hell of an arm. Leroy was laughing until he saw the man whom she had "maced" get to his feet. He had a very familiar revolver in his hand.

That's my old heater.

"Shit!" Leroy said as he made a grab for the guy and the gun. He couldn't touch the man, but he was able to grip the gun. He focused his energy into the pistol, trying to make it unable to fire. However, affecting the living world was nearly impossible. He tried to jam the barrel or throw off the sights. He tried to fill the gun with his essence as the angry man pointed it to the now-fleeing woman as she ran towards the stairs.

Leroy felt the hammer cock and the firing pin hit the bullet. He felt the explosion as if it were inside of him. The hot lead was a part of his soul, torn out and fired from the barrel of the gun.

It was glorious, burning agony. He pulled at the part of his soul that had become the bullet veering it off course. He felt it hit her. Yanked from a killing shot, it became a glancing shoulder wound. She screamed and fell, rolling heavily down the stairs.

"You fucking killed her, man! What the hell's wrong with you?!" the man with the broken nose said as he finally got to his feet.

"Shut up, let me think," the blurry eyed man said, trying to catch his breath.

Leroy's spirit energy transferred from the pistol up the man's arm, filling him with dread. The world was suddenly full of nightmares and all of them were coming for him.

The lights flickered three times before they came back on. Shouts could be heard outside. His courage gave out and he dropped the pistol.

"Let's get the fuck out of here!"

The men stumbled over themselves to get out of the house, cursing and swearing as they ran into the street.

Leroy knelt down next to the woman. He knew she wasn't dead, but she was hurt. "Hey . . . come on, Sweetheart . . . Don't do this . . . Get up, ok," he pleaded. "Open those peepers . . . Come on . . . wake up."

Iris felt a slight fog in her head as she heard Humphrey Bogart whispering to her. She slowly opened her eyes and tried to sit up.

Pain lanced through her as she tried to move. She could feel a dull ache in her hip and shoulder, but other than that, she barely felt anything.

I am lying on the floor. The ceiling could use some dusting.

A man came into view, looking down at her in concern. He was in a suit and tie that looked like he had slept in. They were slightly wrinkled, and the tie hung loose. He didn't have the jacket on, and his sleeves were rolled up to the elbow. The top button on his collar was undone.

His dark curly hair was slicked back from his face. It was a ruggedly good-looking face with a days-worth of stubble, like he had forgotten to shave this morning. She stared up at his very intense eyes.

"Oh . . . hello . . . thank you," she whispered, trying to smile a little. "You must have come because of all the noise. I tried to call the police, but the phone didn't have service."

Leroy whispered in surprise, "You can see me? Hear me?"

Iris nodded slowly. "Yes, you're fuzzy . . . I don't have my glasses on, but yeah. My ears are still ringing, but I can hear you."

Leroy frowned. "You are going into shock . . . You need to call the police . . . Take out your phone. Try again," he said urgently.

She frowned at him and pulled the house coat closer to her. She dug the phone out of the pocket, swaying slightly as a wave of dizziness hit her.

She hadn't noticed the blood dripping from her arm. Leroy frowned and hoped she didn't until she was able to call.

"No signal," she said wobbly.

"Ok, what's your name, Doll?" he asked quickly. He reached out to steady her, but it was like trying to hold up Jell-O.

"Iris . . . Porterfield. It's nice to meet you . . . What's your name?" She was getting confused.

"Iris, go call on the phone—the landline, the old rotary phone."

"That thing works?"

He nodded, and she stumbled to the desk and picked up the receiver. The dial tone blared in her ear. It took several tries before she was able to call 9-1-1. She mumbled incoherently to the woman on the other line before darkness swallowed her up.

Leroy pressed into the wound, trying to slow it down. There was little he could do but keep her in her body and whisper to her.

"It's ok, Iris, you are going to be fine. Help is on the way." He glared out the door to where the two men had fled. The living world . . . It was so much more urgent and frightening. The threat of death wasn't such a threat on the other side of the veil. Here, the stakes were much higher. He needed her to live. He sighed and looked at her pale face. He didn't want her to die, not because of something he did.

It took an agonizingly long time for the medics to arrive. Leroy followed along, riding with her to the hospital, worry and helplessness twisting in his gut the whole way.

Chapter Eleven

Iris woke to the burning smell of vinegar. She winced and tried to move her nose away.

"Easy, easy. She is coming around. Can you hear me? What's your name?"

Her vision was blurry, but she realized she was in the back of an ambulance. An EMT was asking a barrage of questions that she tried to answer. His repetition of those questions told her she was failing.

"She is in shock."

They buzzed around. She couldn't follow what they were doing. Without her glasses or her contacts, they were brightly colored blurs. As nausea hit, she stopped watching until his face hovered into view again. His blue eyes were full of worry.

She smiled at him and shook her head. "It's ok, I am fine. Don't look so worried."

He smiled. He looked funny for an EMT. His face was scruffy, and he didn't have a face mask on.

"You just keep them peepers open, ok, Doll? It's important to stay awake right now." His accent reminded her of those old movies. She smiled and felt a giggle bubbling up. She wanted him to say Humphrey Bogart's line, "Here's looking at you . . . Kid," from Casablanca.

His face drifted out of view again as the other EMT flashed a light into her eyes.

The next few hours turned into a series of men and women in nurses scrubs flooding in and out of focus, asking the same questions. She was put in a hospital bed and given IV fluids. Her arm was examined, poked, x-rayed, prodded and eventually stitched. Police came and took her statement. They said they had investigated the "scene of the attack." Her phone and purse were finally brought to her.

She was forced to call Mr. Bartley's home at three in the morning to verify with the police that she was supposed to be at the office. He was very kind and gave the police a thorough dressing down for not taking better care of her. Mr. Bartley offered to let her stay at a hotel instead, but she gently refused. He assured her new locks would be installed first thing in the morning.

It was almost dawn when she was finally given some peace and quiet. She was going to be released later in the day. The nurses stopped occasionally to check her vitals.

She was dozing off and on when she became aware of someone standing in the far corner. Her eyes were heavy, and her brain was sluggish.

"Oh, I'm sorry, I didn't see you standing there . . . Is there something you need?" she asked out of reflex and deeply ingrained manners.

"Oh, no, Sweetheart, you get some sleep. We can talk in the morning."

Between her pain meds and exhaustion, she had no room to argue. Her eyes closed and she slept.

Leroy kept watch as Iris fell back to sleep.

Mouse wasn't kidding when she said I wouldn't like it.

Many of his colleagues back in the day thought dames couldn't handle themselves. He had always known better. Women were more dangerous than men.

That didn't mean it was right to put them in harm's way, certainly not for his own gain. He was furious. Mostly at himself. *She had fought hard.* He could feel her fear, but she had still gone after those guys. Brave and foolish. She was just the kind of bravehearted idiot that would do what he needed her too. And *damn it,* he didn't hate it.

You're a real bastard, Leroy Mahoney.

He had no respect for men that took advantage of women and children.

Yeah, I know. I am a piece of trash. But I am going to rescue that girl no matter what.

He moved and sat on the edge of the bed. He could feel a fragment of the bullet still in her arm. Some tiny sliver of it with his energy stuck inside. That was their connection. It was why she was so clear to him, and he to her.

The tether was still fragile. If he reached in right now, he could yank it out, and the connection would disappear. That would have been the decent thing to do. But it wasn't what he needed, and he wasn't going to. He gritted his teeth as he watched her sleep.

"I'm sorry, Lady. But I can't save the kid without you," he whispered as he reached out towards her. He concentrated on his energy and slowly pushed his hand into her body. It was like shoving his hand into warm pudding. He found the seed of the spiritual tether and pushed his energy into it.

As their connection grew, a burning sensation increased.

She didn't even stir in her sleep. The pain was all Leroy's. He yanked his hand away, holding it against his chest.

"Well, that should hold long enough for us to get this guy. So, get better quick. We've got work to do," he muttered before sitting in the visiting chair to rest.

Chapter Twelve

Iris woke to her phone ringing. She groaned; her body ached, and her head throbbed. She sat up, holding her arm to her chest. Everything hurt this morning.

"Hello?" she answered without looking at the screen.

"Oh my god! What happened!" Vanessa's voice boomed out of her phone. "You were shot! I am on my way there! And I am bringing your monster cat with me," she continued to practically shout. Iris slowly shifted in the bed, letting her feet dangle off the side.

Iris opened her mouth to protest but stopped.

"Are you really?" Her voice was a whisper in the room. She wanted her cat, and her best friend there. But she didn't want to push or be a burden. Years of trying to do everything on her own made asking difficult. She hugged herself a little as she tried to push the residual fear aside.

She looked down at her knee and winced at the dark bruises forming. Her hip and shoulder told her how they had fallen down the steps. The fleshy part of her butt also protested. Today she was grateful for her extra cushioning curves.

Vanessa, unaware of Iris's self-inspection, continued speaking, "Yes, I am driving to you as we speak. Don't worry, I have you on speaker phone."

Iris smiled softly and relaxed. "Please tell me you didn't say anything to my parents."

Vanessa scoffed. "What am I, new? God no. I am glad you put me as your ER contact. Or god only knows what would've happened."

Iris sighed. "Ok. Good. I can't wait to see you. I am going to go back and get cleaned up. Drive safe and don't forget to give the cat food and water while you are out. Love you, Vanessa."

"Love you, too, Sweetie. I will see you later today," Vanessa said before she hung up.

Iris sighed and put on the pair of scrubs they had given her. She was glad they had her size, though they stretched tight over her hips. She put on her glasses as she gathered up her meager belongings and put them in her bag, which she promptly dropped as she turned and saw a man sitting in the chair across the room.

Her face flushed as she realized she had been changing with someone right there. Her eyes wide, she was so flustered she didn't say anything. Her brain glitched as she tried to process.

He is smoking! IN the HOSPITAL.

He just sat there watching her as if he had all the time in the world. A thin trail of smoke rose upward from the end of the short cigarette.

"Excuse me!" she finally managed to get out.

He quirked a brow and the side of his mouth twitched up slightly.

"Oh, no . . . No excuse needed, Doll."

She frowned as she looked around. She recognized his

face but had no idea where he had come from, or why he was in her room.

"What are you doing?" she said, keeping her voice down. She didn't know why she was whispering. She shouldn't be embarrassed; it wasn't her fault that there was a strange man in her room. But her instincts were almost always to hide first.

He shrugged and got smoothly to his feet.

"Waiting on you, Sleeping Beauty," he said as he flicked the cigarette away. Her eyes tried to track it, but it disappeared out of sight. Iris glared at him as she considered calling security.

A flash of memory popped into her head, and a hand flew up to her mouth in surprise.

"Wait, you were the one that found me. After I was attacked." She wanted to be grateful for his help. However, his not saying anything while she was changing didn't sit well. *I am too tired and sore for this right now.*

"Thank you for your assistance. And in the vein of being grateful, I won't report you for watching me change." She did her best to keep her poise and dignity, though all she wanted to do was hide.

He smirked a little. "Oh, you can if you want to. It won't do you any good. No one else can see me so I wouldn't recommend it."

Iris heard his words and considered him carefully. He seemed confident and relaxed. *Ok, Iris it is a very real possibility that you are in a room with a seriously delusional individual. Let's not agitate him.*

She smiled and nodded.

"Yes, of course. Well, I suppose I won't then. Have a nice day," she said as she turned and headed for the door. It was best never to argue with crazy people. She glanced over at him one more time and ducked out.

Leroy watched her go, taken aback by her quick shift in demeanor. He had expected a bigger reaction. He put his hat on and followed her through the door. She was making good time down the hallway. He kept his distance in the hospital because he didn't want to cause a scene here with her.

She can't help me if she is put in a loony bin.

Though he figured when this was all over, she could chalk it all up to trauma from the attack. He felt a little guilty for watching her change. He had meant to say something sooner, but the words just hadn't come.

Not sure what that says about me. Besides, she had her back to me. I barely saw anything. He pushed the guilt away as he walked out of the building. Iris was climbing into a car, so he sat on the trunk as it started to drive. He rode and smoked another cigarette.

If he closed one eye, he could see the spirit world zipping passed him. If he closed the other, he saw the bright living world. It was a strange feeling. He knew it was about concentrating on one side of the veil or the other. He had never had a bridge before. The living world was much more intense now that he was dead. *I get why a soul would possess the living just to feel anything again.*

Though, it took a strong spirit to possess a living person. Leroy had heard of skin riding before, where a spirit would slide just along the inside of a person. They had no control, but they had all the sensation. Whatever that human was doing—eating, showering, driving—they would experience it with them. It was dangerous because it was easy to forget who you were. Some who did it too often would completely lose themselves afterwards and start to fade.

Leroy had always assumed that someone became a skin

rider because of their weak will or a personality defect. At this moment, he could begin to see the appeal. He shook his head clear of those grim thoughts and slid gracefully off the back of the car. It had pulled up to his office. He was surprised to see that the building was almost the same on both sides of the veil. Pride filled him up as he headed into his office.

Iris came in a few minutes after him. He honestly expected her not to even show.

Who would want to go back to the place where they almost died? . . . Well besides me.

He could see she was upset. Standing stiffly in the doorway, fidgeting, her eyes wider than they needed to be, she sucked in a deep breath. After a three count, she let the breath out in a rush.

"Enough, Iris. This is stupid. In or out; you're not a cat," she said in a firm voice.

He smirked at her self-pep talk. It worked because she stepped inside and closed the door. Keeping her gaze away from the mess the intruders had made, she didn't see him as she went up to the apartment.

Maybe she can't see me all the time. Do I have to do something to allow her to see me? Leroy wasn't sure how all this connection business worked. Yet another thing he would have to figure out as he went along. He followed her up the stairs. *I bet she is throwing everything into a bag and running home.* Leroy reached the top of the stairs and was surprised.

She isn't cleaning . . . Is she cleaning?

One by one, she washed the few dishes in the sink and then scrubbed down the countertops. After that she pulled out a bucket and some rubber gloves from a cupboard. She put her hair back, gathered up a soap and a bristled brush, then headed back down the stairs.

He watched in quiet amazement as she scrubbed her own blood off the floor.

What kind of person comes back the day after being attacked and cleans their own blood off the floor? She is still in the clothes from the hospital.

Leroy knew what it took to do something like this because he had done it a time or two himself. However, he had always been told there was something seriously wrong with him.

This Powder-puff is made of tough stuff. He had expected waterworks fear, outrage. He had never expected her to come and do this. Maybe he was behind the times.

"Dames sure are different these days."

At the sound of a man's voice, Iris let out a tiny squeak and then a pained gasp as she slipped. Her already bruised posterior sent a sharp bolt up her back in protest when it connected with the hardwood floor. She looked around the empty room.

What at first looked like a smudge on her glasses formed into a person shape, and a man slowly came into view. He leaned relaxed against the wall.

How did he get there, he couldn't have reached that corner without passing me. Iris sat with her ass on the wet floor, her heart pounding in her chest. It wasn't until her need for air burned her lungs that she remembered that she needed to breathe to live.

He stood there, part of him still transparent, as if he hadn't finished coming into focus yet. With a smile, he moved forward, each step making him more solid. When he reached Iris, he crouched down in front of her.

"Hey, Doll, you look like you have seen a ghost. Finally." He grinned and wiggled his eyebrows at her.

The absurdity of the situation and his awful pun caused a giggle to bubble up and escape. It was quickly followed by a squeak and a laugh. Iris slapped a hand over her mouth and looked away from him.

"Nope!" she said forcefully. "No, no, no. I refuse . . . I am not doing this. I am not seeing this. They aren't real," she said as she righted herself a little, picked up the soapy bristled brush, and continued scrubbing the floor. "You have just had a traumatic experience and have taken serious medication," she said firmly.

"Aw, don't give me the cold shoulder. This is my place after all. Though, I guess it's not fair that you have to clean up." He moved closer, forcing himself into her view again. "I would help if I could . . . but as you can see." He demonstrated by passing his hand through hers.

"What are you doing?" She flinched away at the strange tingling sensation left behind from his touch.

"Now, don't go get all ruffled. I was just trying to show you that I mean no harm. Can't even touch ya," he said, holding up his hands.

She frowned because she had felt him. *Didn't he feel it too?*

Up close, she realized she had seen him before. He was smiling from the black-and-white photo on the wall in the office.

"Are you supposed to be Mr. Leroy Mahoney?" she said quietly, staring at him.

"Supposed to be and am, in fact," he said with a laugh.

"You don't look like your picture," she said skeptically. The man in the picture seemed sharper, meaner . . . scarier somehow. "It's far more likely you are a hallucination concocted by my brain. A mix of my trauma and the medication. After all, I was reading one of your novels when

I fell asleep before the attack." She shifted her posture and tried again to focus on her task. She pretended he wasn't there and went back to cleaning, using towels to wipe up the last of the water.

Mr. Mahoney—it seemed too personal to think of him as Leroy—smiled at her and waited. He gave her a full three minutes before he leaned forward.

"Do you often take me to bed . . . to read?" he whispered close to her ear.

Iris blushed to the roots of her hair, her eyes going wide, as she gave an embarrassed sound. "That is not what I meant!"

He was already moving back towards his desk, drawing her into the office and away from her task.

"Why did they bring all the boxes up here?" he asked as he looked around.

"They didn't. I did," she said in a slightly annoyed tone.

"Why would you haul all my stuff up here?" His gaze snapped over to her with a narrowed eyed, sharp look. "You didn't buy the place, did ya?"

She shook her head. "No," she assured him.

Mr. Mahoney quickly continued his questions. "Then why are you pawing through my personals?"

She tried not to get irritated. "I am the appraiser and account auditor."

He turned and looked confused. "Audit? How can a dead man get audited? IRS change the rules again or something? Not surprised, honestly."

Iris shook her head, knowing she shouldn't indulge in her own delusions. "Not you. Mr. Bartley is auditing his estate and getting his affairs in order. He is well onto ninety and wants to make sure things are taken care of after he passes."

Mr. Mahoney nodded slowly and gave a dramatic sigh. "I don't want him selling my place."

Iris folded her hands in front of herself and answered in a carefully crafted and practiced, polished tone: "Of course not. But as you are no longer the owner of this property, it would fall to the executor to determine what would be best for all parties concerned."

Mr. Mahoney looked at her and shook his head. "I may have died but this was my office. My life. Not some name on a piece of paper. And Eugene would never do that."

Without realizing it, Iris had begun cleaning up. The thieves had made a mess, tossing papers and items everywhere. Iris crouched, pulling them back into a neat stack. Putting the chaos back into order helped her feel in control.

"I don't know why I am arguing with my imagination. I am here to perform the audit, make sure no one has been stealing from his accounts, and help determine the value of this collection. I won't be discussing this any further."

She did her best to ignore Mr. Mahoney as he moved about the room. *Why wasn't he disappearing?* Maybe she should go back to the hospital? No, she just had to get through the day. Vanessa would be here soon, and everything would be fine.

Leroy watched as she cleaned up the space. He was surprised how carefully she was handling his belongings. As she touched items, flashes of memories came to him. Where the items came from, and the cases they were connected to. He smiled as he watched his life play in snapshots.

His thoughts turned to Eugene. When Leroy had first gotten stuck in the in-between, he had checked in on Eugene. Back then the newlywed had been doing alright for himself. Leroy took some time to look at the photos that had gone up in the living world since then. Yeah, it looked like Eugene had done alright for himself.

Leroy took a seat and waited. He figured he should let Iris get the space into order. It was going to be hard enough to force her to realize he was real. Not to mention that, it was about to get a great deal worse for her.

Chapter Thirteen

IRIS HAD FINISHED CLEANING up the office. She had sorted the stacks of papers and objects she had been reviewing. Now she stood, frowning at the neat little rows and stacks.

"Your face will stick that way," her imaginary companion said from where he lounged near the window, twirling his hat. She didn't respond to him but tried to concentrate on what she was doing. She counted them again.

"Ok, uncle. What is it that you are so upset about? You have counted them like four times; the number isn't going to change," he said, as if he were getting irritated at her. Her delusion had some nerve, to say the least.

"That's exactly the problem," she said angrily.

"Come again?" he said as he appeared next to her.

"It's the exact same," she said by way of explanation.

"Yeah, so. It's all my stuff." He nodded, not getting what she was driving at.

She looked at him like he was thick. "I thought you were supposed to be a good detective," she grumbled.

He looked irritated at her. "Hey, Lady, I am trying to be patient with you. Don't go busting"—the light came on—"

Oh. You mean the *same* . . . they didn't steal anything. Maybe they didn't get a chance."

She frowned and shook her head. "That's what was weird. They were searching for something. The man said, 'Where is it?' They were here for something specific." She sighed and tapped her lip as she looked around the room. "But what on earth could it be?"

Leroy shrugged. "My guess, it was something of yours. All this stuff has been here for ages. They had years to dig through it. Why wait until there was clearly someone here and run the risk?"

She considered that. "If it was mine, why did they dig through your boxes? They didn't even bother with Mr. Bartley's side of the room . . ." They both looked over at Bartley's desk. It was sitting almost completely undisturbed.

"Good point." Leroy looked around again. "So maybe it wasn't because they wanted something; maybe it was more about making sure you didn't see it."

She nodded. "That's a possibility. Maybe to hide assets? Or perhaps they had hidden something here for safekeeping, like stolen goods, and didn't want it to be put up for appraisal because it would have been recognized." She sighed and shook her head. "I don't think they took anything so at least that's something."

Iris smiled as she picked up the cleaning supplies to take them upstairs and then get herself cleaned up. Vanessa would be here soon. Iris didn't want her to see the mess.

Leroy nodded but made a mental note to come back to this little mystery later.

"Look, Miss Iris. We need to talk," he said, trying to get to the work at hand.

Iris rolled her eyes as she went up the stairs. "No, we don't. I realize this is a subconscious part of my brain trying to get me to process the events of last night and make them into something easy for me to cope with."

Leroy groaned. "No . . . I am Leroy Mahoney, and I need your help." He got to the top of the stairs. "I am dead. I am a ghost. And we need to shake a leg and get a move on."

She washed her hands and started putting coffee on. "Why would a ghost need my help, and why would he be in a hurry?" she muttered as she headed back towards his bedroom. At the door, she stopped and pointed at him.

"You stay there," she said firmly as she closed the door in his face.

Leroy stopped in his tracks. *Cheeky dame. It's my bedroom. When was the last time I had any woman in there?* He tried hard to banish that thought, and then the water in his shower turned on.

"Is she trying to kill me?" he grumbled as he sat down at the counter.

When he sat down, his mug of steaming coffee appeared in front of him. Taking a sip, he lit his cigarette and smoked quietly as he listened to the sound of his shower. His mind traveled back to the last time he had a lady here.

He tried to remember her face or her name. He was sure her hair was brunette. Not chestnut brown, but that dark brown where it was almost black. Though he couldn't remember anything else about her. As the coffee brewed, the faceless memory nagged him.

"You're still here." Iris's voice sounded unsurprised but a little disappointed. "Look, I have someone coming, so I want you to leave before she gets here." Iris came out. She was dressed with her hair loosely wrapped in a towel. *I wonder what her shampoo smells like* . . . He shook the thought clear. *Now is not the time, Leroy.*

"Iris, I am working a case. My client is a young girl named Lucy. She was stolen. More precisely, kidnapped. We need to find her. I can do that, but I need to get her locket. I can use it as a compass to her location."

Iris watched him as she finished putting her coffee together. She made a little noise in her throat as she took a sip and nodded, like she was listening. He waited a moment before he continued.

"All I need is for you to pick it up for me and bring it back here."

Iris smirked around her cup. "Why do you need me to do that, exactly?"

Leroy gave her a glare. "Because I am a ghost and can't pick it up."

She raised an eyebrow and shook her head. "This is ridiculous. I am not going to go on some locket adventure just because a hallucination says so."

Leroy groaned. "I am not a hallucination." He could feel himself getting angry. He knew it wouldn't help, but it was there. He needed to do something. He had to help Lucy. Which meant he had to convince Iris he wasn't a figment of her imagination.

He frowned as he considered how to do that exactly. However, Iris seemed to be a step ahead.

"If you want to prove you are a ghost from the 1940s . . . Then you need to tell me something that I would have no way of knowing. Something that only someone who was there would know, but I can verify." She had a smug little smile.

Something in his expression must have given away his confusion.

"You are, without a doubt, the worst hallucination ever." She turned and headed towards the couch.

He smirked and took a moment to appreciate the sight of her in leggings and a sweater. "I have been called worse."

"But that's my point, you haven't. You are just a figment of my imagination. My brain is taking information I have gathered here and forming you up as some strange coping mechanism. But because you are formed out of my own mind, you will only know things I know or I have seen."

Leroy frowned. *What is with her?* He was getting tired of this nonsense. He didn't want to play games with this dame, but he needed her to cooperate.

"So, if I can prove that I am Leroy Mahoney, here beyond the grave, you will help me?"

Iris rolled her eyes and waved a hand. "Fine, fine. If you can prove that you are Leroy Mahoney, the dead detective coming from beyond the grave to ask for my assistance, then yes, I will help you."

He grinned and picked up his hat. "I'll take that bet."

Chapter Fourteen

Iris watched "Leroy" put on his hat. He was tall and good looking. His shoulders were broad and squared, but he was all lean muscle. It was the kind of strong that managed to not look intimidating, handsome without it being overwhelming. It was like her mind was using her favorite things. She didn't like being so easily played. *Stupid brain, is this because of Brenden and my impending break up?*

She liked Leroy's face. Though his attitude could use some adjusting.

It took a few minutes, but then finally, he smiled.

"Ok . . . you want something no one else knows about. That you can verify after all these years." He grinned. "Follow me."

She nodded and motioned for him to lead the way. He walked right through her. She felt that tingling again, only this time all over her body. It was a strange sensation, cool and invigorating. It made her shiver. He must have felt it too this time because he stumbled slightly and had to take a moment to steady himself.

"Sorry about that . . . haven't spent much time with the

living since . . .," He mumbled as he headed to the bedroom. She could hear his footsteps on the floor.

Iris followed him slowly, trying to remain calm. It had been a long time since she had any hallucinations. And none had ever been so detailed. Few had ever talked. She didn't want to go back to the constant doctor visits and medications like before.

She followed and watched as he tried to move the bed. For some reason the floors creaked beneath him, but he couldn't move the furniture.

He swore in frustration.

"Ok . . . You get it. Under the bed, there is a loose floor-board. Get the box that is inside."

Iris sighed as she knelt. Being careful of her hurt shoulder she pushed the bed to one side. It didn't take long to find the floorboard with Leroy's direction.

"It's a good thing this floor hasn't been redone or you would have lost this place for good," she muttered as she used a nail file by the bed to pry up the board.

In a mass of dusty cobwebs was a small metal box. It reminded her of an old lunch box or a tobacco tin. She gently pulled it out of the floor and frowned, blowing the dust off the container. It wasn't large, about the size of a small shoebox. She set it on the bed and he gave a whistle.

"Wow, that is dirty. Guess no one ever found it after all." He laughed and rubbed his neck. "I always kinda assumed Eugene would find it." He seemed to snap back into the present. "Here is the plan. I am going to tell you what I remember being inside. And if I am right, then I have proven I am Leroy Mahoney," he said with a grin. He put his hat on at a funny angle as if preparing a magic trick.

Iris had to squeeze her lips together very tightly to keep from smiling. He was such an odd character. He looked like he would be a hard-boiled detective, cynical, rough, and rude. But he had this boyish charm that made it seem almost fun.

"So, there are a couple letters from a Sweetheart I had while I was in the war, a deck of cards that a lady shouldn't be looking at, a wad of cash, and some baseball cards. Probably some other odds and ends that I stored there because they were valuable." He waved his hands over the box and winked. "Ok, Doll, open her up."

Iris laughed despite herself and pried the lid off. The tin had been sealed tight. It had done an excellent job of protecting the items inside.

Leroy grinned, watching as Iris pulled the lid off his old tin can. Inside, sitting right on top, was the deck of playing cards. A woman with beautiful dark-brown hair and lovely large, exposed breasts was laid out across a fluffy-looking blanket. The queen of hearts had barely faded. He felt embarrassment fill him as he looked at the blush forming on Iris's face.

She cleared her throat delicately and gingerly moved the cards to one side. Below the risqué ladies were several very neatly stacked and tied letters. All were addressed to Corporal Leroy Mahoney. She was frowning now as she took out the baseball cards and then a couple of strange coins he collected overseas. The last thing she pulled out was a small ring box. Leroy gasped and jerked forward to stop her from opening it.

"No—that's private," he said forcefully. His hand was more inside hers than on it, but it stopped her from opening the ring box.

She looked up into his face. Her skin seemed impossibly

warm and pink compared to the pale grey of the people he had grown accustomed to.

"Is it enough yet, do you believe me?"

She blinked and nodded slowly. He didn't understand the expression he saw in her eyes. *Why does she look so relieved?*

"Yes . . . I believe you. I just don't understand how, or why," she said, finally returning the items to the tin.

Leroy relaxed a little as she set it down.

"Well, it's a bit of a long story so let me just sum it up. I need you to help save a kid." He sighed as he took off his hat. "Normally, I would never involve a lady such as yourself, but at the moment, you are my only horse in the race. So, I have to bet on ya." He pulled out a smoke and lit it.

Iris frowned and waved a hand at the smell of the smoke. *That's new, how can she smell that?* She got up and opened the window. She stood there for a long moment.

Since she wasn't speaking, Leroy decided to continue, "All I need from you is help getting a locket out of an old, abandoned building. Once I have the locket, I will be able to track the little girl and get her to safety, and I will disappear and this will have all been a trauma-induced hallucination, just like you want."

She stood with her arms crossed, looking out at the city for a long time.

"Get you a locket, and it will save a little girl? That doesn't even make sense," she grumbled.

Leroy laughed. "It doesn't need to make sense. It's the world in-between. The little girl needs her locket. Or do I have to be a pest forever?"

She looked at him and he gave an open-armed gesture, letting her know the choice was hers. Now, it wasn't really true: he couldn't haunt her forever. At least he didn't think he could, but she didn't need to know that.

She sighed. "How far away is this locket?"

Leroy smiled; he had her now. "It's just a few blocks. An hour of time, tops. Easy peasy."

She looked at him suspiciously. "I won't break the law. I am not going to jail." She headed to get her coat and shoes.

"No, no. Nothing like that. No one lives there now."

With a resigned sigh, she put on her coat. She wanted to get this over with before Vanessa arrived. "Why do I feel like I am going to really regret meeting you?"

Leroy smirked and put on his hat. "You wouldn't be the first, Sweetheart."

Chapter Fifteen

IRIS FOLLOWED Leroy as they made their way down empty streets. The late evening and wet weather kept almost everyone inside. She tried not to complain and trudge through it. Maybe she was crazy for agreeing to do this at all. But maybe he was telling the truth, and it would just go away if she completed a stupid little task.

There was a small park that looked like it had fallen into ruin ages ago. The swings were broken, dangling on rusted chains. The seesaw looked like it hadn't moved in years. The grass was overgrown, and the trees were either wild or dead. There was a strange musty smell in the air like rotting leaves. She pulled her coat tighter as she walked.

This totally looks like a place people were murdered.

They approached an old stately house. Its porch had begun to sink in the middle and droop on the sides, giving it a sort of grimaced mouth. The door was shut with a large no trespassing sign nailed into the wood. The storm shutters had been closed for a long time. Some of the panels had come down from the windows. It caused the eyes of the house to have wild pupils dilated at different sizes. The paint had once been a lovely blue but now had faded to a sickly grey. The yard was yellow and brown.

A faded for sale sign was planted in the front yard. Iris knew anyone who saw this place would never buy it. It wasn't abandoned, or even condemned. It just felt dead.

It was the corpse of the home it had once been. There were signs that at one point, someone had loved it and tended a garden in the front. Bits of dead rose bushes still clung to the garden area. The delicate gingerbread trim around the eaves was beginning to fall off. The death of the house seeped into the ground around it.

Outwardly, there was very little wrong with the place. Nothing new windows or a fresh coat of paint wouldn't fix.

Iris looked at the other houses in the area. It seemed like a nice neighborhood. Their colors were vibrant. Their lawns were green and full of flowerbeds.

The yard of this house was larger than the others on the street. The other homes sort of leaned away from the dead house. It took Iris a moment to realize why it seemed that way. It was because the homes next door had been built farther away on their lots. As if the buildings themselves didn't want to be near it.

Iris completely agreed with the sentiment. She stood on the sidewalk across the street from it and shook her head.

"No. No way. I am not going in there," she whispered to Leroy as he stood next to her. "I am sure it's not safe. It says "No trespassers.""

"The locket is inside. I would get it myself, but I can't pick it up. Besides, the creatures there are too dangerous for me."

Iris snapped an angry look over at him. "Creatures? What creatures? You want me to go someplace full of *monsters*? Why would you send me into such a dangerous place?"

Leroy sighed. "The monsters in there are in my world. Interacting with the living world is very difficult for the things on this side of the veil. Because you and I are connected, I can see the living world. And you can see me. They shouldn't be able to reach you," he said in a soothing voice.

Iris shivered as she looked at the building again. "Shouldn't?! I don't want to go in there by myself."

Leroy nodded as he considered the situation. "There is a way I can go with you if you want. But I am not sure you are going to like it."

Iris looked at him suspiciously. "So far, I haven't really liked any of this. What is it?"

Leroy smirked and adjusted his hat. "You're just going to have to take me for a little ride. But don't worry, Sweetheart, you ain't the first woman I've been inside of."

Iris blushed to the roots of her hair, heat rising from her chest and neck. "Excuse me?!" she sputtered in outrage.

Leroy tipped his hat back a little as he watched her reaction and an embarrassed smile played across his lips. "Sorry, Doll, I forgot how that sounds." He laughed as she glared at him.

Iris was not amused. She took a moment to collect herself. "Ok. Fine, let's do this."

He grinned and gave her a wink. "Alright, let's shake a leg and get this done."

Iris sighed and nodded. "Yes, please. Let's get this over with."

Leroy concentrated on the fragment of the bullet still embedded in Iris's bone. His energy focused down so that he was protected within her body from the monsters outside.

Using their connection, he focused on seeing through Iris's eyes. It was far easier than he had expected. He was surprised by how much he could feel. He could feel her emotions like fear, and her excitement. He could feel the physical things like the cool breeze on her cheek, and the heat of her embarrassment. He experienced them as if they were his own.

It was strange to feel small and vulnerable. He hadn't felt that since he had been a small boy. It did help him understand a little about why she was so hesitant. He couldn't imagine what it was like to have had to fight two grown men in the middle of the night, feeling so small and delicate. It increased his respect for her determination.

He tried to help her feel his confidence. "Don't worry, Iris, I'm with ya. We got this."

Iris moved across the street. She had to go around to the back door. It was damaged and easily pushed open. She paused before she slowly went inside.

Leroy could feel the chill in the air. The sense of foreboding that seeped into her skin. He could feel her breathing pick up and her heart rate quicken. He heard the creaking and groaning of the house. He knew that the creatures in the spirit world were watching her, trying to reach her. Their presence still had an effect on the living world even if they weren't able to breach the veil.

He could feel her fear starting to bubble.

"Don't do that," he whispered to her. "They will feed on your fear."

She shivered a little, tiptoeing through the darkened inside. The air was cold and dank. The rooms and hallway were suffocating with dust. Light seeped in through holes in shutters and the broken windows. It was weak and grey in comparison to the sunlight. She shivered and rubbed her arms as she walked through the living room. The furniture was covered in large drape cloths

"Where am I going?" Her whisper was muffled in the gloom. She took a deep breath and squared her shoulders, trying to be brave in the creepy atmosphere.

Leroy smiled inwardly. "Attagirl. Alright, it's down the hall, on the left, in the back bedroom."

Iris walked slowly down the hall, pulling out her phone to use as a flashlight to see in the dark. The farther back they went the worse the damage became. There were bits of broken glass and maybe ceramic plates on the floor. It looked like someone had taken an ax to the place. Splintered wood and metal stuck out of the wall like sharp teeth trying to reach for her.

"Be careful, you don't want to cut yourself in here. Once the blood leaves you, it can serve as a connection to whatever is lurking here on my side," Leroy cautioned her.

He felt her nod to him. She picked her way carefully through the hall and jumped when a loud banging came from above. The spirits haunting the building were trying to make her afraid.

"It's ok, Iris. I am here with you. You can do this." He tried to give her a sense of calm and confidence.

She reached the end of the hall and moved into the bedroom. Neater than the rest of the house; it was as if this place was off limits to the destruction that was prevalent else-where. The window was intact, and the floor was free of debris. There was a bed tucked in the corner, an old dresser against one wall, and even some shelves remained on the wall. The faded wallpaper had the room being blue.

Iris spent some time looking at the room. "I think this was a little boy's room," she said finally.

Leroy frowned as he looked around. "Why would you think that? There isn't anything personal here." He felt her muscles move as she motioned to the wallpaper. "That is faded but

it looks like spaceships." She walked to the windowsill and pointed. "Yeah, see, there is a named carved into the wood. It looks like Charlie."

Leroy smirked a little. "I knew a lady that went by Charlie."

Iris sighed and shook her head. "I don't want to know about it. It's just a feeling, that's all."

Leroy grinned as he felt her irritation. Keeping her calm was more fun than he expected it to be. Her being embarrassed or irritated helped keep the fear at bay. If it worked to keep her going, he didn't mind teasing her.

"It's over there behind the dresser. Maybe feel back behind it or something."

Iris nodded and moved over to the dresser. She tucked her phone in her front coat pocket so the light shined out but was secure. She shifted the dresser, trying to look around it. She knelt carefully down and looked under it. "I don't see anything."

He sighed and could feel the connection to the tether. "It's there. Pull the dresser out and look behind it."

Iris sighed in irritation. "Fine." She grumbled as she got back to her feet and started trying to move the dresser. Leroy fought a grin as he felt her straining against the heavy furniture. With a grunt, she was finally able to get the old wood moved enough to look behind the dresser.

I need to remember she is only five foot five. I am lucky she isn't one of those delicate tiny ladies or she might never have gotten this thing moving.

Once moved it revealed a smooth, clean wall.

Iris frowned and pulled her phone out of her pocket to flash the light around it. "That's weird."

Leroy looked at it with her and nodded. "Yeah, it is. It's tucked in there somehow. I can see the glow from the wall."

Iris moved closer and ran her hand along the space until she felt the tiny crack in the wallpaper.

"I found a seam," she whispered as she leaned down and used a key from her pocket to pull the opening free. Shining the light in, she found a strange wooden box. Once she pulled the cloth-wrapped box out of the hole, she stood up and rested it on the dresser. Leroy watched as she unwrapped the box. It was about the size of a shoebox, and the old wood looked hand-carved. It opened easily, and there among the cluttered interior was the glint of the golden locket. Leroy grinned and gave a sharp whistle.

"Great work, Iris. Grab it, and let's get out of here."

Iris was not focused on the locket. She was looking through the other items in the box.

"This is weird," she whispered softly. "That is a man's watch, and a woman's bracelet. There are a bunch of driver's licenses, and an engagement ring? Though none of this is terribly valuable. I can't even figure out why all these things would be together. This isn't exactly a proper safe. It's just a hidden hole in the wall. And why would a little girl's locket be in the little boy's room?"

Leroy sighed in frustration. "Who cares? Just get the locket and let's go."

Leroy could feel the moment Iris realized something was wrong. She looked around the room again. "This room is clean. It doesn't have any of those drop cloths. But there is no dust. I think someone has been in here recently."

Leroy tried hard to bring her back on track. "Even more reason for us to get what we came for and get out."

Iris pulled out the locket. She frowned as she held it up in the light. A dawning horror shaped in her mind as she looked back at the things in the box.

"There is blood on the locket. Why is there blood on the locket Leroy?" she whispered.

Leroy felt her fear, her revulsion. He knew the moment the understanding of what she was holding took root in her thoughts.

"Don't think about that, Iris. Just grab it and let's go." He kept his voice steady, hoping to keep her courage up long enough to get them out safely.

She shivered as she looked at the other items, ignoring Leroy's urging.

"There's blood on this too. Why is there blood, Leroy?" she asked, her voice raising with urgency. She swallowed a hard lump in her throat as the answer formed in her brain. "This box doesn't belong to the little girl. Does it?" Her voice was a trembling whisper.

Leroy considered not answering for half a heartbeat but finally said, "No, I don't think it does."

Iris swallowed back the bile that had started to burn in her throat. Anger was taking over the fear that had been filling her up.

"This belonged to whoever killed her. This is the murderer's box."

Leroy wasn't sure if he preferred her smart or not. "Yeah, I am pretty sure this is where he collected his trophies. We need to get moving, Iris."

He felt rage radiate through her like the heat of a campfire.

"Are you telling me you sent me into this haunted monster house to dig around in a serial killers murder stash!" she shouted. He felt it echo through him, making him flinch.

She cursed under her breath as she shoved things back into the box. Leroy sighed in relief. *As long as she takes the locket and puts the stash back, everything will be fine.*

"Just put the box back, Iris, and get the hell out of here," he encouraged her.

The box was wrapped back up and almost into the wall when she stopped.

"When did Lucy die, Leroy?" Iris's voice was steady.

He flinched; Iris had never used Lucy's name before.

Leroy frowned, watching her hands holding the box in midair. He tried to push her to put it in the wall. She didn't budge. A bad feeling came over him. No matter how much he pushed, he was just a passenger.

"Like a week ago, maybe less. Why?" he replied cautiously.

Three heartbeats passed as dread filled Leroy. Suddenly, Iris turned and headed out of the room, holding the box tightly to her chest.

"What are you doing?! Put that damn box back in the wall!" Leroy shouted at her. She ignored him as she hurried out of the building.

"Why are you taking the murder box, Iris!" he said, freaking out as he heard the creatures from the house howling in rage. She had just stolen their tethers.

She didn't answer until she was safe across the street, where she began shoving the box into her purse and walking away through the park.

Leroy appeared next to her, looking at her and following along half a step behind her. "What the hell are you thinking?"

Iris stopped near the broken swing and looked over at him. He was brought to a halt by the look on her face. Fear, determination, anger, hope. Her face was so open at that moment it was almost painful to read.

"If she died last week, that means he is still out there. If she died that recently, it means all those people are dead and the police haven't found him. I need to figure out how to get this to the police so they can try and catch this asshole before he murders some other little girl." Her words tumbled out in a rush.

Leroy nodded slowly. "You're right. Ok . . . calm down. Just take a breath," he said. She was panting heavily like she was about to have a panic attack.

Iris nodded and took some deep breaths. Finally, she grinned up at him. "We can stop him, Leroy. We can do this. I just know it!"

Leroy winced. It was worse than a panic attack. She was exhilarated. The only problem was that stopping a serial killer was not what Leroy was doing. It certainly wasn't something he should try to do, even when he was alive. That was the job for the police, the real police, not some accountant and a postmortem private eye.

Hell, even what he was doing now was beyond the bounds of what was allowed. Helping her catch a living killer was meddling in the living world. That was trouble with a capital *W* for Warden.

He had to tell her that it was never going to happen. He fidgeted with his hat and ran fingers through his hair.

He finally looked, at her. He had never seen her smile. She had dimples on both sides of her cheeks. Her eyes were huge in her face. The excitement had her cheeks flushed. If Leroy's heart was still beating, it would have skipped one.

"Come on, Leroy. Help me stop this guy."

But how was he supposed to say no when she looked at him like that? He let out a sigh of resignation and frustration at his own weakness.

"Yeah, ok, Iris, but we have to be careful."

Iris beamed up at Leroy before she started walking again.

"I can't believe I did this. This is so crazy!" she said. The excitement was still pulsing through her system. Her mind was buzzing. She grinned at the absurdity of it all. "I have no idea how I am going to explain finding this . . ." Her words trailed off when she looked back and Leroy was gone.

Iris stood alone in the park. Her smile faded as she scanned the open empty space. A cold breeze ruffled her hair. The air was quiet but heavy. She could still make out the house across the park. A deep unease settled in her bones.

"Leroy?!" she called out but only the wind called back.

Feeling exposed and vulnerable, Iris turned and hurried away. She didn't stop until she reached the office. She made it back in half the time it had taken her to reach the park.

She hadn't been running, but she was panting by the time she burst into the office and slammed the door behind herself.

"Leroy?!" she yelled as she walked and looked around the main office. Her concern was growing. The box seemed heavier now that she was on her own. "Where did you go, Leroy?" her voice was small as she stood next to his desk.

There was no answer. The late afternoon sun had finally managed to burn off the heavy cloud cover and flood the room with light from the big bay windows. The office was warm and inviting, making the dark little box more gruesome in comparison.

"Iris? Is that you?" a feminine voice called from up the stairs.

Iris realized who it was almost instantly. "Vanessa?" she called, turning towards the stairs.

Her dear friend was already heading down with a big smile. She stopped at the bottom of the stairs, and a large fluffy grey cat lunged past Vanessa and into Iris's arms.

"Bogart!" Iris gasped, ignoring the pain catching him caused. She happily snuggled the big fluffy cat. Vanessa didn't wait and instead just wrapped her arms around both.

After a big hug from everyone, Vanessa stepped back and smiled curiously. "So . . . who is Leroy?"

Chapter Sixteen

Vanessa sat thinking, sipping coffee and staring at the items on the counter. In the center was the murder box, to the left of it the gold locket, and to the right the photograph of Leroy.

Bogart purred calmly in Iris's lap as she waited for Vanessa to respond to everything that had just been explained. Vanessa had been Iris's friend since they were both little kids, and they never kept secrets from each other. They were closer than any sisters Iris imagined would be.

Vanessa rubbed her temple before letting out a long sigh. She took a moment to collect herself before she looked at Iris. "Ok, let me just make sure I have this straight. You took the job so that you could get out of the city and away from a certain someone. And while you were working the audit, you got attacked by two masked men. After the attack, the ghost of Leroy Mahoney came and convinced you to go and collect the locket of a little girl that was murdered. Which just happened to be in a terrifying haunted house, stored in a murder box of some serial killer. And instead of putting it back and running for the hills, you took the box with you? Because you think you can give it to the cops and help them catch a killer?" Vanessa said it all very concisely, and though she didn't use a judgmental tone, Iris felt very small as the insanity was laid out clearly.

Iris nodded as she looked down at the top of Bogart's head.

Vanessa reached over and opened the locket. On one side was a picture of an adorable little girl, and the other was a smiling couple. The family resemblance was clear. "She sure is a cute little girl." She smiled a bit and looked up at Iris.

"First question, is Leroy as good looking in person?"

Iris smiled and gave a little laugh. "You don't think I am crazy?"

Vanessa rolled her eyes. "Oh please. How long have I known you?"

Iris shrugged. "My whole life basically."

Vanessa nodded. "Don't even get me started. I have always believed you saw ghosts when we were little. I knew you weren't crazy. You have never been fanciful. You were always honest and level headed. If you say it was a ghost, it was a ghost."

Vanessa smiled encouragingly and gave Iris's hand a squeeze. "Now we know for sure. How, else do you explain finding the box? Hidden in a house you have never seen, in a town you have never been in. It's either ghosts or your psychic."

Iris blinked back tears and sighed in relief. "It feels strange. I know getting the locket was the goal, but he said we would work together to get the killer. Then poof, he was just gone."

Vanessa frowned a little as she looked at the photograph. "He was old Mr. Bartley's partner, right?"

"Yeah, why do you ask?" Iris looked at her curiously.

"Well, I was thinking maybe you aren't the only person he has visited. Wouldn't he go see his old partner first?" Vanessa replied as she considered the box again.

Iris thought about it and finally nodded. "Yeah, that would make sense. Maybe we should go talk to him. He used to be a detective; he might know what we should do with the box too. Or should I just call the cops?"

Vanessa shook her head. "No way. What if they think you are the killer?" Iris gave Vanessa a skeptical look, and Vanessa laughed a little. "Ok, fair enough, you don't exactly give off killer vibes. How would you explain finding it? Are you planning on telling them ghosts were leading you? Or that you broke into someone's empty property for kicks and found it?"

Iris frowned as she looked at the box. "Maybe I can send it to the police anonymously. I don't know."

"That's why we should ask," Vanessa said sagely, then drank her coffee

Iris nodded. "I will give them a call and see if we can stop by this evening. I have some other things to ask him about for the audit anyway."

Vanessa grinned a little. "Look at you . . . Turning into a detective all on your own. This is going to be fun. Best vacation ever!"

Bogart meowed and looked completely unimpressed.

A few hours later, Vanessa pulled into the long driveway at the Bartley's.

"Wow. I haven't seen a place this big in a long time. This is crazy. He got all this writing detective novels?"

Iris laughed and shook her head. "Not just detective novels. He writes all kinds of fiction. He just got started with mysteries."

They waited to be let in. Julie once again answered the door.

"Welcome back, Miss Porterfield. I am so glad you are alright. Eugene was hoping to speak with you."

Iris smiled as she came in and nodded. Vanessa walked quietly behind them, looking at the warm, cozy decor as they took a seat in the parlor.

Once they were all seated in the soft, comfortable chairs, Julie brought in warm cups of tea. She sat down and joined them.

"He will be down later. He is resting right now. Is there anything else I can do for you two?" she asked.

Vanessa smiled and shook her head. "No, thank you, ma'am."

Iris tilted her head as she thought for a moment.

"Julie, how long have you worked with Mr. Bartley?" she asked quietly.

"Oh, I have worked here for over twenty years now. Mrs. Bartley hired me. After her passing, I stayed on as Mr. Bartley's main caretaker."

Vanessa grinned over her teacup and wiggled her eyebrows. "Oh, that sounds kinda romantic."

Iris gave Vanessa a look and shook her head. "I'm sorry, she is a hopeless romantic."

Julie smiled and nodded. "Well, there was a bit of romance once. But only briefly. It shifted to two friends keeping each other company. After a while, we found a routine here."

Iris raised an eyebrow in surprise as the nurse continued, "The truth is, he never stopped loving his wife. He misses her every day. He talks to her often."

Vanessa leaned closer. "Like her ghost? Does he see her?"

Iris gave Vanessa a sharp look.

"Oh, her ghost isn't here. She moved to the beyond many years ago, but he talks to her anyway. It helps him stay settled."

Iris frowned a little. "I am sorry, what do you mean, to the beyond?"

The nurse smiled. "Oh, I am sure, you understand. I can see it in your aura. You have been connected to one yourself." She took a sip of the tea.

Vanessa and Iris shared a surprised look.

"Wait, you can tell she has been talking to a ghost?"

The nurse smiled knowingly. "Not just talking to, Miss Porterfield. You two are connected. I see some of the energy still hanging around you. It wasn't there the last time you were here. Who are you seeing?"

Iris blushed heavily and sipped her tea. "It is Leroy Mahoney."

The nurse burst into a bright smile and nodded. "Oh Mr. Mahoney. I heard so many stories about him. I have sensed him at the office many times."

Vanessa smiled. "Have you ever seen him?"

The nurse shook her head. "Oh no. I can't speak to ghosts. I just can tell when they are hanging about. Did he show up to help you during the attack?"

Iris gave a shy nod. "Sort of, he said he came for a different reason, but he did help when I was attacked."

Julie smiled and took another sip. "What did he come for, then?"

Iris looked at Vanessa, who nodded eagerly. "Come on, who else is going to believe us?"

Iris sighed, and with a resigned look, she pulled the box out of her briefcase. She gingerly set it on the table.

The nurse recoiled from the box immediately, her face grave and pale.

" . . . That is a very bad box. You best tell me all about it."

Iris sighed and nodded. Julie sat back and solemnly listened to her explanation.

Chapter Seventeen

LEROY BLINKED as light filled his vision. One moment, he had been following behind a very excited and adorable Iris, and the next, he was trapped in a black void, not at all sure he even still existed. There was no pain, sound, just a big oppressive nothing. Time had lost its meaning. He couldn't move or escape. Just trapped.

The light that appeared was blinding. When he was finally able to see, he was sitting in front of a very angry-looking Warden.

Jack leaned on the black-and-white wall. Michael, the Arbiter, sat across from Leroy, glaring at him. To Michael's left was a female figure with skin like the night sky. It absorbed the light and turned it into pinpoint stars inside her feminine form. Leroy had never seen her before.

"Well, hello, Mike . . . long time no see. Where is Goldie?"

"Not long enough for me, Leroy. And Goldie's busy. Tell us about the girl," Michael replied stiffly.

Leroy gave a cocky smile. "Oh, Mikey boy, gentleman never kiss and tell." He didn't know what the Arbiter was after, but Leroy knew he didn't want to give it. The Arbiter had been looking for a reason to rip him to pieces for years. Goldie was his biggest gofer.

A searing pain roared along Leroy's body as if flames had been injected into his skin.

"I have no time or patience for your games today, Leroy. Tell us about the girl."

Leroy gasped as the pain stopped. He glared at Michael. "I don't know what the hell . . . you . . . are . . . on . . . about," The pain started before he even finished the sentence. It took Leroy a huge amount of effort to grit the last few words out.

"The female you were with."

Leroy frowned in confusion. "Damn it, Jackal. Why are you just standing there? The girl got ripped right out of my hands. What more do you want to know? She was just a kid that was killed. I was helping her cross just like I always do."

Michael slammed his fist on the table. "Not her. The living one. You know the rules: forced possession is forbidden. It is a high crime to take over the mind or body of another!"

Leroy glared at Michael. "I didn't possess anyone. Forced or otherwise."

Michael scoffed. "Really, and how did you get her to go into that nest of monsters to retrieve your client's locket?"

Leroy smiled smugly as understanding dawned. *He is pissed. I figured out a loophole, and he doesn't know how. Sorry chump, today is not the day.* "I asked her nicely."

Michael glowered at Leroy before turning to the woman next to him. She nodded. "He speaks the truth. He did not possess her and asked for and received consent."

Michael snarled and stood up. "You stay away from the living, Leroy. You tread over that line, and I will find a way to return your essence to the ether!"

He vanished from the room with a painful vibration of energy and light. Jackal sighed and approached Leroy.

"Michael has never gotten along with Eshu or his children. He doesn't approve of your dance with Fate. You swim in the deep grey, Leroy. Best be careful so you don't drown in the blackwater."

Leroy tugged his jacket in place and shifted in his seat. "Don't worry, Jack. I am being very careful. I have no interest in oblivion. The connection that was created is only temporary. And the mortal has not been tricked or coerced. She was glad to help."

The jackal shook his head. "That can sometimes be worse, my friend."

The face of the starlight woman turned towards Jackal. "What are we to do with him?"

Leroy frowned. "What do you mean? You need to let me go. I gotta go find the kid before it's too late. Not to mention, I need to make sure the little bird doesn't get dead while I am away . . . Hang on, how long have I been in here anyway?"

Jackal tilted his head. "You know that time here is relative, Leroy. It only matters if you make it matter. And here, it doesn't matter at all. As you said, you were the nearest to the girl when she was taken. You saw what happened."

Leroy was confused. "I told you what I saw. A bright light, searing heat, pain, and a terrified little girl. It happened too fast; I couldn't see anything else."

Jackal smiled. Which was not, on the whole, a pleasant thing. His maw opened and his glistening canine teeth peeked out over the blood-red tongue. He huffed and licked his snout and clacked his jaws. He often did this when he found something amusing.

"Leroy, what did I just say about time? What is an instant, but an eternity?"

He leaned forward and his dark eyes met Leroy's. "We

have figured out a way to search for the thief. Most souls are not strong enough. They would be torn apart. But you are different. You will endure. You will help us."

The starlight woman reached out and took ahold of Leroy's arm. "This will be unpleasant," she spoke softly.

Leroy had just a moment to be concerned before it began. It was unpleasant. Oh yes . . . Very.

Leroy had no way of knowing how much time had passed. There was only pain. The moment in his mind when he watched Lucy being snatched was pulled and stretched and paused. His face contorted in the agony while they peeled away layer by layer until they had all been analyzed.

Leroy wasn't looking at the moment; he was in it. He was stuck in that horrible instance, trapped in the pain and terror. They had to strip it all down to its most basic essence in time. He was trapped there so long Leroy started to forget there was a different time, or a different place. He began to forget what he was looking at. He was becoming lost in the space of this moment.

Just when he was sure he would never escape, there was a break-in the burning flames. Through them, the face appeared. The man who was pulled a terrified Lucy from Leroy's hand. In that instance, that face would be etched in Leroy's mind forever.

Chapter Eighteen

JULIE LISTENED to Iris's story. She was frowning deeply by the time they came to the end of it. Then they all sat in silence as they sipped lukewarm tea and considered what she had gone over.

"My, that is unusual. I have heard of some people developing strong connections to the otherside after a near-death experience. But that does not seem to be the case here. And even in those cases, to be able to fully see and interact with a spirit in this fashion is just downright bizarre." She puzzled over it while she nibbled a cookie. "I know a lady in town. She is more connected to the otherside than me. We'll call her and bring her over right away. She may be able to help protect you," she said as she rose.

Vanessa frowned a bit over her cup. "Protection? From Leroy?"

Julie smiled and waved a hand. "Oh no, not him. The otherside is as vast and full of dangers as this side. There are those that prey on the unsuspecting and the vulnerable."

She dialed a number and spoke to a woman named Edith.

Iris leaned over to whisper to Vanessa, "I am not sure how comfortable I am with her calling anyone. I feel like too many people know about this as it is."

Vanessa waved a hand. "Don't worry, I am sure it will be fine. Besides, we still need to talk to Bartley about what to do with the box and figure out where the heck your ghost boyfriend went."

Iris practically choked on her tea. "Oh god, please don't call him that."

Vanessa grinned teasingly. "It's cute. That should totally be a thing."

Iris shook her head vehemently. "No. No. It is definitely not a thing."

Vanessa nodded. "Yep, totally a thing."

Iris took a deep breath, trying to find her center and to not get frustrated.

It took about thirty minutes for Edith to arrive. She was considerably younger than Iris had expected her to be. Iris had thought she would be some old gnarled-looking woman. Perhaps like the witches she had read about as a little girl. But Edith was in her midforties with long, rich, dark hair, and striking green eyes. She walked with purpose. She wore a comfortable-looking off-white linen suit. She pulled behind her a travel case on wheels with a little handle. She reminded Iris of those traveling makeup artists that her mother hired for events.

Edith had a warm smile for Julie as she walked into the room.

"So, this is the young lady I was talking about." Julie motioned to Iris.

Iris stood and held out a hand in her most professional manner.

"Good evening, Edith. It's nice to make your acquaintance."

Edith smiled and took the offered hand, simultaneously enclosing it with her other hand. A delicate silver bracelet around her wrist jingled and caught Iris's attention. She felt an intense heat spread up her arm for a brief second and then a sudden head rush. Edith steadied Iris and helped her back to her chair.

"Ah, there you go. Relax, it's ok. You had picked up quite a load there. I find it best to clear the air before I talk shop with anyone." Edith spoke in a soft, tone as she moved to sit across from Iris.

Vanessa looked concerned and brought Iris a fresh cup of tea.

"What do you mean, a heavy load?" Vanessa asked.

"Well, to be completely frank, your friend seems to have been playing in some rather dark places. The creatures of the otherside cling to the living. They can leave stains, if you will. They crave the warmth of life, the memories and feelings of the living. Their touch can leave behind remnants of themselves. The burden can be heavy. It weighs on everyone differently, but it presses down on us."

Iris sighed as she considered this. "I do feel better. It felt very hopeless a moment ago. I feel a little more like myself."

Vanessa smiled and rubbed Iris's shoulder. "That's good. You look a little better too."

Iris gave a faint smile. "Thank you, Edith."

Edith nodded and took the cup of tea that Julie handed her.

"I will leave these young ladies in your care, Edith. I have to go see how Eugene is doing." Julie turned and smiled at

Iris. "You are in good hands. If you are done before I come back, just leave the tea and I will clean it up later."

Iris nodded. "Yes, of course, ma'am."

"Thank you, Julie. I will see you later." Edith waited for Julie to leave and then turned her attention back to Iris.

"Alright, Iris, so why don't you tell me what you know, and let's see what can be done about it."

Edith listened quietly as Iris explained the events in as much detail as she could manage yet again. She sipped her tea and asked simple questions. At the end, the silence stretched out unbearably for Iris. They had eaten all the snacks and drained the pot.

Finally, Iris couldn't take it any longer and blurted out, "Was Leroy trying to hurt me?" Iris tried to sound calm, but her voice had a little squeak to it.

Edith blinked and came back to the present. "Oh, Dear. I am sorry. I was communing. I didn't mean to worry you. No, no, Leroy Mahoney isn't a danger to you. The connection between you is quite safe." Edith set down her cup and pulled her case over to the table.

"Sometimes when a spirit attaches themselves to the living, it is to siphon their energy or emotions. But this is very different. He has anchored a part of himself inside you so that he can communicate to you, and you can call to him."

She began sorting out little glass jars and carefully packed items.

Iris watched Edith, both curious about the objects in the case and impressed with the professional and organized look of her setup.

"Well, if he is anchored to her, why isn't he here now?

Why did he suddenly disappear?" Vanessa snarked, deeply offended on Iris's behalf.

Edith didn't hesitate to answer: "Something on the other-side is preventing him. It could be any number of things, including entities from that house."

Iris frowned as she considered that. "You mean he could be in danger?"

Edith nodded as she set out a few candles and an incense burner as well as a few coins and some other odds and ends.

Vanessa scoffed. "Wait, he is a ghost. He is already dead; how much danger could he possibly be in?"

Edith sighed and put a soft cloth of silk with sigils and runes carefully stitched into the fabric across the table. "More than you realize. There are many things on the other-side that feed off the essence of the human soul. They consume it, use it, and enslave it. But the living have the benefit of dying to escape. The dead do not. That is why they have so many guardians."

Iris felt panic begin to rise up her throat. She swallowed hard and clenched her fists. "How do we help him?"

Edith's hands stilled as she looked up from her work. "Help . . . him?" She gave Iris a penetrating look.

Iris nodded and leaned forward. "This was terribly important to him. He went through all this trouble to reach me so that I could help save Lucy. He wouldn't just leave when we were so close to helping her. Something must have happened . . . . Can we do something for him?" Her words came out in a rush.

Vanessa grinned looking at Iris's flushed and earnest face. "Yeah, we have to save Iris's ghost boyfriend." Iris gave an annoyed glare at Vanessa.

Edith studied her for a long moment, ignoring Vanessa's teasing. "This is a very dangerous idea, Iris. You have no experience and no protection from the things waiting on the otherside. He should never have involved you. I can try and cut the tether that connects you to Leroy and help shield you until his anchor fades. You should anonymously give that box to the police and forget about all of this."

Iris stiffened as something deep inside protested the very idea. She wondered if that was the anchor Leroy had left or it was her own stubbornness. Taking a moment to consider what Edith was saying, she looked at the box. It was dangerous and full of the evil that had created it. The golden locket sitting on top glittered, claiming Iris's attention.

"No," Iris said much louder than she intended. Flushing, she looked down at her hands, trying to soften her tone. "I am sorry. No . . . I can't abandon Lucy. She needs help, and Leroy can't help her without me." Iris straightened her spine and squared her shoulders. "I will help him. I would greatly appreciate it if you would tell me how I might be able to do that." Iris held Edith's gaze steadily.

Edith's smile sent a shiver down Iris's spine. Vanessa tensed slightly beside her. They both waited for Edith to speak.

"Excellent. I am glad to hear that, Iris. The first step is to retrieve your dead detective. He seems to be in a bit of a bind." She leaned forward. "You will have to go to the otherside and retrieve him. I can help you."

Iris swallowed her fear and nodded. "Send me there how?"

Edith began setting up crystals and other strange objects in what seemed to be designated places on the silk. "Your spirit will leave, cross through the veil, and bring him back. It's a simple thing. Not easy . . . but simple."

Iris paled but her resolve didn't shake. "Ok. Simple."

Vanessa reached out and took Iris's hand.

Edith smirked. She set out candles and her mortar and pestle. "It's good to be afraid. This is dangerous and will have lasting consequences. Are you sure you want to do this? Once you start on this path, there is no turning back."

Iris frowned as she looked at the strange altar that Edith seemed to be building on the small coffee table. She turned and looked up at Vanessa's worried face.

Vanessa gave Iris's hand a squeeze and tried to look reassuring. "I am with you either way. You must do what is right for you. I know you can handle it."

Iris smiled and nodded. "Yes. I can do this. Let's get started." She looked back at Edith.

Edith struck a match, but the flame was blue and didn't smell anything like sulfur. The light it cast across Edith's face momentarily contorted it. "Yes. Let's begin, shall we?"

It didn't take as long as Iris expected to get set up. There were trappings of the mystical, candles, and incense crystals, but it was far simpler than she would have thought. Edith took out a scented oil and painted it on Iris's forehead. The lights seemed to dim in the room. Iris sat back on a comfortable chair with her feet up.

"Just relax, Iris, it will be like a dream. You will slip in, and in the form of a shrouded figure, I will guide you there and back. You will be perfectly safe."

Iris nodded and closed her eyes, breathing in the sweet and thick smoke deep. It weighed heavily on her skin, like a warm blanket. After a moment, she felt like she was floating. First, she bobbed in the warm water of a bath . . . then an endless pool. The darkness was filled with stars. She floated on until the moon drifted down from the night sky and hovered in front of her.

Iris reached out her hand and took a step forward, and

the heaviness left her limbs. She was weightless, calm and peaceful. Her bare foot touched cold stone and she looked down.

The twilight world spread out before her.

Iris gasped in wonder at the beauty of it all. Lights and shadows danced with each other. A whole city spread out, swirling with activity. Suddenly there was a figure standing next to her. It was just a humanoid shape. Their face was shrouded in a black smoke, but light filtered from behind it. The rest of them draped in a cloak of flowing twilight.

"We must hide your light, or they will know you are a visiting soul." The voice was a mix of two voices at once: one deep and rough with a faint growl, the other high and silky, full of sweetness. The figure covered Iris in a hooded cowl of the same black smoke. Iris felt a strange sense of ease and calm. Her eyes told her she should fear this thing, but her heart was completely calm. *They won't hurt me. They won't let anything hurt me.* This truth carried itself in her mind, transforming everything into an adventure.

Iris smiled and nodded. "Ok, where do we go now?" Her voice sounded strange to her ears, like a faint echo of what it normally was.

"This way. Where you go isn't for the faint of heart. Prepare yourself."

Iris nodded as they moved through the city.

It was a mishmash of different time periods. She watched as people from all different eras strolled past. Some looked as solid as anyone else on the street. Others were transparent and barely there. There were walking corpses with horrible wounds and others that glowed with a shining little light inside of them. Terrible creatures walked alongside little children. The denizens of the city were as varied as nightmares and daydreams. She stayed close to her guide, peeking at the world of the dead from beneath her hood.

Time didn't touch here. It certainly didn't affect how they traveled. One minute they were walking down a long street, then blink, they were somewhere else completely. But the walk across the courtyard took forever. She didn't complain since she wasn't tired. Her feet didn't fatigue at all.

The courtyard led to a police station. An old police sign hung above the doors as they slipped in. No one noticed them as they walked past the uniformed officer at the desk. He was dozing. They followed a few hallways and down a flight of stairs. Whenever anyone would come up the hall, Iris and her guide would pause.

The figure in front of her held a finger over their mouth area to ask for silence.

They finally came to a door that said, "Interrogation 1." Iris peeked in the window. There was Leroy sitting across from a man and a woman. They were almost frozen in time. His face was contorted in a mask of agony. The other two seemed to be meditating.

"What do we do?" Iris finally asked.

The figure gave a shrug. "My duty was to bring you here and take you back safely."

She considered the window. "I need to get him out of there." She looked further down the hallway. It was as much a mishmash as the rest of the city. At the farthest end of the hall was a number of cells. Groups of strange-looking people were pacing or sitting in the cages. Iris spied a set of keys sitting on a desk at the front of the cells. She considered the consequences for a moment but decided to move.

As fast as Iris dared, she snatched up the keys. The shrouded figure watched her with interest as she moved to the doors. As quickly as she was able, she unlocked them. It never crossed her mind that it was odd that she knew exactly which key to use. She simply did, and as she threw the final lock, she ducked out of the way and hid as the prisoners bolted out. There were howls and shrieks and she covered her ears at the horrific sounds they made. The air froze and burned in turn as they rushed by.

When the noise moved away, she peeked up out from under the desk. An alarm sounded and shouts began down the hall. She was about to move when a black cane barred her path.

A tall man with a black silk top hat stood in front of her. The silver-topped cane he carried tapped slightly on the ground. His black skin gleamed in the dim light, drawing attention to his perfect pearly-white teeth. Eyes like hot coals burned as he leaned forward to peer under Iris's hood. She swallowed her fear hard and took a step back as he grinned at her.

"My, my, my, what an interesting turn of events. What a lovely thing you are. I won't forget you, my little flower. You can be sure of that." He laughed and Iris was very sure she didn't want him to remember her at all.

Her shrouded guardian stepped forward and the top-hat man put up a hand.

"Don't fret, don't fret. Just taking a peek," he said. He turned and vanished into a shadow.

Iris shivered and moved back to the interrogation door. The man and the woman that had been in with Leroy were already chasing down escaping prisoners. Iris made sure they were out of sight before opening the door. She slipped inside and the Shroud followed her.

Leroy had his head down on the desk. He looked exhausted and sweaty. She hadn't realized ghosts could sweat. She reached out and carefully touched his head.

He flinched back suddenly, his eyes wide.

"Who is there?" he barked as he looked around.

The Shroud whispered, "He can't see you with the hood up."

Iris nodded and pulled the hood back.

Leroy gasped and jumped to his feet. "Iris! What the hell?" He looked confused and then looked at the Shroud. "Why are you here?"

Iris frowned. "I came to get you . . . We can talk somewhere else . . . They are gonna be really mad at me if they catch me."

Leroy frowned and grabbed his hat. "Why would they be mad at you?"

Iris sighed. "I may have opened all the cells down the hall."

"YOU DID WHAT?" he shouted, grabbing her hand.

"I had to get them out of the room and keep them busy so they wouldn't notice you were missing," she said unapologetically and grabbed his hand in return.

Leroy frowned as he jammed his hat on his head. "We will be discussing this later." He muttered under his breath, "Crazy dame."

The Shroud moved along with them as they turned down a slightly different way than they had come in.

"How do we get out?" Iris asked both of them. The Shroud nodded and pointed to the left. They followed him quickly, avoiding the way the other prisoners were running. They moved through several other departments before coming out a side exit into an alleyway.

They walked a few blocks before Leroy turned towards Iris. "Ok, hold onto me," he said as he picked her up into his arms and suddenly raced through the streets. The world became a blur.

The wind whipped past them as they sped through dark alleys, and narrow causeways. She thought that they would go back to his office, but he took her to the other side of town. They stopped in front of a set of old-looking buildings.

The streets were narrow and crowded. Red paper

lanterns hung on the front awning. He set her on her bare feet and took her hand.

"Don't let go of my hand," he whispered as he headed through the door. A black raven was painted on the front. Iris nodded as she followed along behind him. He stepped through, and the inside was lit with a warm glow, but it was still dark and full of little booths with privacy screens.

A tall boney woman dressed all in black feathers stood next to a narrow desk. It was made of gnarled and bent wood with a huge book perched on top of it. She looked up, her eyes completely black and beady. Her elongated face was sharply pointed with a wide mouth that turned into a smile.

"Mahoney . . ." She winked at him, and they seemed to have some kind of understanding because she nodded and passed him a large, heavy key.

"Return the key when you're done," she said and went back to her book.

Leroy smiled and nodded. "Thanks, Doll."

He led the way up a narrow, twisting staircase to the very top. There was a short, curved door. Iris was the only one who didn't have to duck to step through.

Once inside, he shut the door behind them and locked it. He sighed and moved to collapse in a chair. The room was surprisingly spacious, with a soft bed and a table with chairs. A window looked out over the city. They were in a dark area, but the lights of the rest of the city were pretty and sparkling. Iris found herself watching the lights move and ebb. They were little rivers or a pulse of electricity moving along the wires.

Leroy looked like he was sleeping so she sank down into a chair and sighed. The Shroud just remained hovering in the corner, waiting.

Iris decided to let Leroy rest. She didn't know what they were doing to him, but she didn't want to add to his burden.

Spotting a blanket at the foot of the bed, she rose quietly and placed it over him.

Returning to the chair, she continued to gaze out the window. She watched as wonders and terrors moved through the streets beneath them. *I am glad we are so high up.*

Chapter Nineteen

LEROY GASPED in surprise as he awoke with a start. Looking around in a panic, relief washed over him as he spotted Iris sitting in a chair by the window. *How the hell had she managed to get here? With a Shroud no less!*

That was some serious protection. He hadn't seen one in a long time. Whoever helped her get here had serious juice. He frowned as he looked her over. She was definitely still alive. He could see her glow even beneath the shrouded cloak. She was looking off at the lights flickering outside. Even with the Shroud, he could make out the curve of her face. He could spend all day looking at her. Iris had the kind of gentle beauty that reminded him of her name. She wasn't a stunner, not forceful in her attractiveness, but the kind of lovely that would withstand the rain.

Leroy tried to shake off those thoughts. *Don't go there, Roy. Nothing there but heartache and headaches.*

If he was making the curve out right, through the shroud she was smiling.

"How's the view?" He hadn't known he was going to speak until his words filled the air.

Iris jumped, a little startled by his voice. She quickly moved towards him, looking him over.

"Never mind the view, how are you?" Her voice was full of concern as she put a hand to his forehead.

Leroy almost laughed out loud. *What does she think she is checking?*

She brushed his hair back off his temples, and he was startled by the sensation of her warm hand against his skin. No one this side of the veil was warm to the touch. He looked at her face.

"I got a fever, doc?"

She blushed slightly and stepped back. "No . . . I was just . . ." She clasped her hands together. "Checking."

He smirked slightly as he moved, heaving himself from the chair to the window. He pulled a cigarette from his pocket and sat on the sill to smoke. He looked at the lights and sighed.

"Well, we certainly caused a ruckus."

She sighed and nodded. "I am sorry about that. But you were gone and then I saw you locked up . . . I wasn't sure what to do."

Leroy blew smoke out the window. "Well, it was slick, bought us some time. We need to move our sticks, or we will be pinned down and cooped up."

She nodded and looked at the Shroud. "Can you get us both out of here safely?"

The Shroud nodded. "Yes. We should go before dawn."

Iris looked at Leroy. "Are you ready to go?"

He nodded and grabbed his hat. "Let's make tracks then."

The Shroud moved forward and took Iris's hands and reached to take ahold of Leroy's arm.

"Fuck me," he grumbled low because he knew what was about to happen.

For Leroy, passing through the veil was not a pleasant experience. It was like running through a wall of fire. He held on tight and grimaced as they reappeared in the living room of his old partner.

Iris was lying still on a chair. Well, her body was, at least. The Shroud evaporated now that its task was complete.

Leroy looked over at the bright glowing form of Iris's astral form. He found himself smiling as she took in the scene. Another woman was seated next to Iris, watching her sleeping form carefully.

Edith was chanting at a small table.

Leroy sneered a little. He really didn't like that woman. *Well, that explains how Iris got across the veil, with a Shroud no less. I can't believe Edith would stoop that low. Even with a Shroud, sending Iris was reckless.*

Leroy knew Edith was good at her craft. They had run-ins with each other before. Some pleasant, some not. Edith often meddled with magic from the otherside, which was why it should have been a simple task for her to remove the anchor.

She must want something from Iris, or me. Better watch my step around that viper.

Leroy's focus shifted as Iris stepped towards him. Or maybe he moved towards her. He couldn't tell. Her warmth flowed around him like the heat of a fireplace. It was so seductive. He wanted to stand closer. It was like he had been out in the cold of winter and was coming into a snug den. Iris looked up at him, completely unaware of his thoughts.

"Are you sure you are ok? You didn't rest very long. And you seemed so tired before." Her eyes were sparkling, and she was so close now.

"Are you worried about me?" he asked, his voice lower than he had intended.

She nodded. Some little devil inside Leroy crept up and gave him a shove.

"Well, there is a little something you can do for me before you head home. If you don't mind." He just barely kept the grin from his face and his voice a low whisper.

She leaned forward just a little to hear him better. "Yes of course, what can I do?"

He leaned in and pulled her tight up against him. Her heat started to fill him. "How about a little boost?" he whispered as he brought his face closer to hers. He pressed his lips to hers, and in that intimate touch, he pulled her energy into himself. It was like pulling electricity out of a battery. It recharged him in a way he had never felt before. She gasped and stiffened against him. He knew she could feel him drawing from her, but she didn't fight him.

It was just a pressing of the lips, but it was enough. A tiny bit of her shine transferred to him. He stepped back and smiled.

"Thanks, Iris, that helped a lot. You're a peach. Now get back into your body before there is trouble," he said to her surprised and indignant face. He had to fight hard not to kiss her again just because of that face.

She tilted her head, and with all the impugned dignity she could muster, she went to where her body lay, sitting down carefully back into herself.

Leroy grinned. *Yeah, she is going to be mad at me, but it was worth it. Besides, those damn guardians really worked me over. I needed the boost.*

The more honest side of his brain called him a liar and said he was just making excuses. He chose to ignore that voice along with the one that made him feel guilty. It told him he better keep his hands to himself.

Iris sat up with a surprised gasp. She could still feel her lips tingle and her heart thump in her chest.

Vanessa moved closer. "Are you ok?"

Iris nodded and smiled softly. "Oh yes, I am fine." She would have to tell Vanessa that Leroy had just kissed her, but not right now with everyone watching. Instead, she smiled and looked at them. "I am sorry you had to stay here for hours. It must have been exhausting."

Vanessa just looked at Iris for a moment.

"Hours? It's been like five minutes," Vanessa said softly.

Edith, who had finished chanting, smiled at them. "Time passes differently on the otherside. A blink of an eye can seem like a lifetime." She nodded and looked around. "I see you were successful at retrieving Mr. Mahoney." She sat back and lit a small cigar from the burning candle.

Iris nodded. "Yes, how did you know?"

Edith shrugged slightly, her linen suit rustling as she shifted back into her chair. "Oh, Mr. Mahoney and I have a bit of history. I have been in contact with him before. I can recognize his energy. It's fairly easy if you know what you are doing."

Iris frowned a little and nodded. Edith smiled, and Leroy watched as Iris's shoulders tightened.

"I take it Mr. Mahoney hasn't really explained that much to you." Edith's voice did little to relieve Iris's tension, and she gripped her hands in her lap.

Leroy groaned and rolled his eyes as he took a seat. "Really, Edith. You don't need to put it like that. You make it sound all sinister. I'm on the up and up."

Edith grinned as she blew out a smoke ring. "Mahoney,

you only have yourself to blame. The girl should know what she is getting into. Have you told the little flower anything about yourself?"

"What did he say," Vanessa whispered to Iris, and Iris quietly explained.

Leroy glared at Edith, though he knew only Iris could see him. In fact, she was looking at him right now, her eyes intense and worried.

"Well, Iris, my partner was hitched to my old flame. And they lived happily ever after." Leroy sank into the chair. "Like I said to him when he proposed, not a big deal. I am happy for them. I even stood with Eugene at his wedding as his best man. As he was heading off for his honeymoon, I was heading back to the office. I fell asleep at my desk and some coward snuck in and shot me with my own gun."

Leroy told the story roughly and abruptly because he didn't want any questions about his little collection of letters or the little ring box inside. Of course, he stood up for his partner. It didn't matter if he loved the dame. Eugene had stepped up and asked first. And Leroy was glad to see him happy.

If Iris remembered his hidden mementos, she didn't mention them.

Edith sighed in annoyance. "We have to figure out what hex was used and get you unstuck. Spirits aren't meant to linger the way you do."

Iris frowned and looked between them. "What do you mean, like a curse?"

"A curse?" Vanessa echoed. In a mutter, she added, "This is as awkward as being the only sober person at a wedding."

Iris winced. "Sorry, Vanessa. I will try to keep you in the loop better."

Leroy was still in mid-conversation with Edith. "You say that, but we tried. I recall you performing all those rituals two years ago when you and that little group were talking to spirits in a graveyard. You were lucky I managed to get all those tethers broken that night, or I would be mad. Some of those rituals hurt. And you still didn't figure out what the curse was."

Chapter Twenty

"I said hex, not curse," Edith reiterated.

"A hex? Isn't that a curse?" Leroy frowned as he waved his match. The smoke rose like a cloud around his face. He half sat in the window of the study.

"Not exactly. A curse tends to be more responsive. May you never find peace . . . May the fleas of a hundred camels nest in your genitals, that sort of thing."

"Oh, I wish that on Brenden! Can we do that?" Vanessa said with a laugh, only half joking.

Iris tried to ignore it but smirked a little.

Leroy looked over at Vanessa. "Who is Brenden?" Iris didn't answer him.

Edith grinned as she moved some of her objects around and tried to get a better reading. She didn't respond to Vanessa either.

"This was a hex. Hexes are personal. They are about intent. They have a goal, a specific thing that they are driven for, and they require a great deal of will behind them."

The smoke from the incense changed color.

Iris looked surprised as she stared at Leroy. "Is someone trying to kill you?"

Vanessa gasped and looked at Iris. "Wait, how do you kill a dead guy?"

Leroy felt a little grin escape onto his face. He covered it by taking a long drag off his smoke. *Why is that so damn cute?* He felt her concern like a warm blanket around him. Their connection was stronger than he expected. He tried hard to stamp out the feeling, to focus. *This connection needs to go.* If he allowed it to root any further . . . He didn't want to think about it.

Once this case is over, she goes back to her life, and I go back to my . . . death.

He tried to look flippant when he snorted and said, "No trying about it, Doll. They snuffed me good." He stood up and flicked his cigarette out the window. "It seems like a lot of nothing from nothing. What's the rub?" He moved to look over the crystals and smoke.

Edith smirked. "Because, you idiot, the hex wasn't there to kill you. It was to keep you from passing on. That's why all this time you haven't been able to cross over. But more importantly, it keeps you from fading." She leaned back. "I still haven't figured out the 'how,' but once I do, I will be able to figure out how to undo it."

Iris frowned. "But why? I thought his unique position gave him an advantage in the afterlife."

Edith grinned and nodded. "Oh, it does, and that was the point."

Iris looked first at Leroy, then Edith. "I don't understand."

"I second that," Vanessa said.

Leroy's expression had turned grim and flat. He tried to keep his voice calm. He hoped Iris couldn't feel his response as easily as he felt hers. "I told you the in-between is dangerous. One of the biggest threats are artificers."

Iris repeated his words quickly to Vanessa before leaning forward to hear the rest.

Leroy sighed and let his fingers pass through the now-blue smoke of the incense. "Artificers use the souls of the dead. They take them and shape them into items of power. They can feed on them, control them. They can use fetters to capture them. It's why passing over is important. They sometimes collect the souls of Shades to make them into weapons and such. That's how currency gets made. The guardians allow specific artificers to collect the pieces of the souls that break free when a soul passes to make currency and substance for those that haven't passed yet."

Edith nodded. "There are some that don't follow those laws. It gives them power in the beyond. This hex was designed to trap you like an insect in sap, to preserve you." She got up and walked to a display case on the other side of the room.

After digging a bit, she pulled out a beautiful small oval paperweight. It was the shape of an egg. It was polished to a high gloss. Edith handed it to Iris, who held it up to the candle's flame. It was a lovely green-and-gold piece of amber. Edith moved and sat back down, and Vanessa leaned in to into look at the paperweight.

"That is a ladybug in amber from the Baltic Sea. That is what gives it the unusual color. That is you, Leroy. You were caught in this hex and left to sit. Now the power has encased you and perfectly preserved you. The most fascinating part is that it allows you to grow in strength but not break free."

Leroy glared at the little egg as if it were to blame. "So what? Get the lead out."

Edith glared at him. "You are the most impatient dead

man I have ever met. Also, the thickest. How did you ever make it as a detective?"

Leroy smirked, adjusted his jacket, and shot back, "A smart mouth and a strong right hook."

Edith rolled her eyes. "The point is . . . whoever did this knew and wanted you this way."

Leroy snapped at her, "And? It doesn't matter. Everyone knows I was done in by a local mob guy because I had accidently found out about his smuggling racket. Eugene caught the guy."

Iris looked at Leroy confused. "That was just in the novel, Leroy. Your murder was never solved. Someone stole your body from the morgue. Eugene didn't know about your death for like months because he was on his honeymoon."

Leroy frowned and gave a grumble. "The truth is stranger than fiction." *Damn it, Eugene. How much artist license did you take with my life?*

Edith grinned as if able to hear that thought. "You know, we could do a spell to help bring back all your original memo—"

Iris's gasp in surprise cut Edith off. She gripped the egg tight. "It means they are coming back."

Vanessa gasped again, this time being cheeky. "Who is coming back!"

Leroy looked over at Iris in confusion. "Yeah, I'm with her, who?"

Edith grinned in approval. "Glad to see someone has some lights on upstairs. You don't go through this much trouble to make a perfectly-preserved-soul battery pack to just leave it."

Leroy scoffed. "That's hokum. It's been over fifty years."

Edith nodded. "True, but this sort of thing takes time. Whoever planned this knew how long it would take and did it anyway."

Iris stood up and walked over to Leroy. "You need to be careful." Vanessa frowned in her seat. "This is really hard to follow because I am missing parts of the conversation, but basically you are saying that whoever murdered and trapped Leroy might come back to use his soul as a battery? Isn't that what they are doing with this little girl?" She looked at the little locket, then at those she could see.

Iris looked back over to Vanessa and nodded. "You're right. We need to worry about one problem at a time. Lucy comes first."

Leroy straightened, fixing his hat and coat. *Everything else can wait; I have a job to do.*

"Standing around bumping gums isn't going to save the kid any faster. I need to get my pillars moving." He moved over to Vanessa and reached out to touch the locket.

Vanessa gasped in surprise as the locket grew cold in her hand.

Iris grabbed her coat and purse.

"What do you think you are doing?" Leroy asked as he saw her packing up.

"I am coming with you, obviously," Iris said as she got her coat on.

"Just cool your heels. Sorry, Doll, as much as I like having a cute kitten following me everywhere, this part is too dangerous. Stay put, and I'll be back around in no time."

Iris's mouth dropped open as her eyes narrowed. "Excuse me? Just who the hell do you . . ."

He was gone before she was able to finish her outrage.

Vanessa looked from Iris to the air. "What did he say?"

Edith laughed and answered Vanessa. "Something very patronizing." Iris huffed and paced around the room as Edith continued, "I mean, for a man from the 1940s, he is surprisingly progressive. He once told me that women were far more capable than men. Something about Fred Astaire and Ginger Rogers."

Vanessa looked thoughtful. "I don't get that reference."

Iris had begun to wring her hands a bit. "Fred Astaire was a famous actor from the silver-screen era. He was an amazing dancer. Ginger Rogers was his equally famous dance partner. It's rumored that when asked which of them was the better dancer, she said, 'I had to do everything Freddie did, in three-inch heels and backwards.' "

Vanessa laughed at Edith's surprised expression. "Oh, Iris is a huge movie buff. She loves all those old movies. I have a closet full of shoes, she has a movie collection."

Iris frowned and looked at the two other women. "I don't care what era he came from. This is not a Bogart movie. I am not some swooning damsel. I am not just going to sit here."

Vanessa grinned from ear to ear. "Attagirl. Let's go!" She jumped to her feet. "But how do we follow him?"

Iris frowned and thought about it before turning to Edith, who was carefully packing up her things. "Do you know how to follow him?"

Edith paused and looked at Iris. "Of course I do. But wouldn't it be better to know where he was going?" She smiled. "You have the locket. He is following the spiritual tether. I could show you, even go with you, if that's what you are asking."

Iris smiled brightly and nodded. "Yes, please, if you don't mind."

Edith grinned and nodded. "Oh, it would be my pleasure. Let's hurry, we are burning moonlight." She quickly gathered her case and the trio headed out the door.

Chapter Twenty-One

Leroy followed Lucy's tether as quickly as he was able. Moving on this side of the veil was very different. The trail glowed with inner moonlight; however, he had flowed along its edge like water running down a line. On the other side of the veil, he would have been able to just flash along its path in blinks. There were only a few other spirits here, and he could feel the drain that it had on him to be here. The connection he had to Iris helped keep him anchored. The spirit world pulled on him. The living world was a sandy beach, and he was waist deep in spirit ocean waves. Sometimes they tugged gently, pushing him back and forth. Other times it was as if he were being dragged away only to get shoved back.

Leroy focused on his job; he needed to get this done and get back to where he belonged. The guardians were already going to be pissed. He didn't need to make it worse by interacting with the living world. Thoughts of Lucy and her face as she was pulled away steeled his resolve. She was counting on him. The end of the tether was at Sophia's Dance Hall. The building was dark, and the doors were locked. The outside wall was painted with lovely swoops and swirling dancers.

He looked at the entrance, and though it was still brightly painted, a small sign read, "Closed until further notice." Leroy could feel a strange pull coming from inside. He wrapped the chain of the locket around his left hand. *I will have to move quick. Just grab Lucy and get out.*

Leroy frowned as he passed through the door into the silent building.

Edith was driving, and Iris rode shotgun while Vanessa asked questions from the backseat. Iris wasn't listening. All she could think about was the pressure building in her chest. Something wasn't right. She didn't know what it was. It made her want to run as fast as she could. Somewhere, anywhere. Sitting still seemed to require all of her attention. Her fingers worried the button on her jacket as she watched the glare of the streetlights pass across the glass of the car window.

It only took ten minutes for them to pull up to a dance studio. The street was empty at this time of night. Edith parked her sedan across from the brightly colored studio doors.

"The spirits you are looking for is in there. Leroy must have already gone inside," Edith said and looked at Iris and then Vanessa. "The place looks like it's been closed for a while, maybe we should wait for Leroy."

Iris shook her head as she unbuckled and grabbed her purse. "I am going in."

Vanessa grabbed her shoulder from the back seat. "For one thing, breaking and entering is still a crime. Not to mention I am pretty sure that the sign over there says 'Police department' on it." She pointed at a grey building halfway down the street from them.

Iris looked at the building and chewed her lip as she considered her options. She was going into that building. She knew that, but how? She had never broken into a place before.

"Maybe we could call in a break-in and have them go check," Vanessa offered after a moment.

Edith gave a little cynical chuckle. "Check for what? To see if a little girl's ghost is in there? And if you did, that would mean it would be even longer before you could go in."

Vanessa pouted and stared out the window. She watched a man walk by. His hair was sandy brown, and he had a nice lean build. He wore glasses and a dark-blue windbreaker. She wondered if he was a college student because of his back-pack, though she noticed the words "Coroner MPD" printed in yellow on the back.

Edith's voice was firm. "It would be wisest to wait here for Leroy and see what is happening."

Vanessa continued to watch the man as he walked to the front door of the dance hall. She grabbed Iris by the shoulder again and gasped.

"Guys . . .," she whispered urgently.

They both froze as she pointed to the door. The man dug something out of his pocket and slipped into the building.

Iris gasped. "He could be the killer . . ."

They all sat silently for a moment.

"Or the necromancer," whispered Edith.

Vanessa nodded. "Or both . . ."

They all looked at each other for a stricken moment.

"If he is the necromancer, does that mean he could hurt Leroy?" asked Iris quietly.

Edith looked concerned and slowly nodded. "Yes."

Iris didn't wait any longer. She opened the car door and climbed out.

Vanessa freaked. "Iris . . . Iris, come on . . . He could be the killer!" she said in an urgent whisper.

Iris looked at Vanessa. "It's ok, I have this." She held up her personal taser. "Oh, what about his magic stuff?"

Edith reached over and handed a pouch to Iris. "Here, put that in your pocket. It will protect you from his magic."

Vanessa glared at Edith. "You *can't* be encouraging this. He broke in; let's just call the cops."

Iris sighed. "Even if we call the cops, that won't help the little girl. Or any of the other spirits he has trapped in there. Look, just give me ten minutes and then call the cops."

She didn't wait for an answer before she quickly crossed the street. Vanessa cursed as she chased after her. They slipped in as quietly as they were able through the unlocked door.

Iris stayed high on the balls of her feet, trying to keep her footsteps as light as possible as she pressed herself against the wall. Vanessa held onto her back as she moved with her. They were moving down a small hallway that opened to a large, sectioned studio. There seemed to be three dance rooms, each lined with mirrors. There was a small front desk in a lobby area. The furniture and desk were covered with white sheets.

The air was full of dust that floated around them, clogging their nose. Iris could see footprints, marking the times that someone with a large-booted foot had passed through. They led straight to the far back dance hall. There was thrumming music and chanting drifting in the air. She could see just the faintest glow. Her heart was thumping in her chest. It was so hard to breathe around the lump in her throat. Vanessa's fingers dug painfully into her back. Iris could feel a chilly sweat sliding down her spine. The taser seemed so small in her hand that she was terrified she would drop it. She moved one tiny step at a time.

I shouldn't be here. I should run. The other hand felt the cold weight of the gold locket.

She bit down on her lip and steeled her nerves as she moved to peek into the dance hall. It had lovely hardwood floors, and one side of the room had mirrors from floor to ceiling. They were covered for protection. All except one section at the far end. The shredded edges of the plastic covering gave proof that someone had ripped it down. In the clean glass beneath, she could see the pair of matching circles. Each had the same number of short candles flickering in unison with their reflections.

Inside the circles was where the difference lay. One had a strange wooden barrel. Not large—it couldn't hold much more than a gallon of liquid, and there were strange markings burned in the dark wood. It was surrounded by dozens of glass bottles of all different sizes and colors, which were all sealed with green wax. The other circle was filled with withered and dried flowers. At its center was a pair of ruby-red low-heeled women's dance shoes.

A man knelt in front of the circles as music played from somewhere in the room. He was looking at the mirror. Iris almost gasped out loud as she saw what he was looking at. In the mirror's reflection, she saw a woman standing in those shoes, pale and sparkling in her matching dress. In the other circle, she saw what looked like a strange glowing vapor rise from the barrel and drift across to the woman. It was like she was breathing it in, gasping for air. Iris saw faces appear in the glass bottles.

It was the spirits he had trapped. She could see that the power that came from those bottles being pulled into the barrel and sent to the woman in red.

The man was chanting as he slowly rose. His

outstretched hand trembled as it met the outstretched hand of the woman in red. Tears streamed down her face as her mouth moved. No words could be heard as he fell to his knees before her, pressing his head to the glass of the mirror.

Vanessa whispered. "What is that weird blur in the mirror? Do you see that?"

Iris felt a tug in her heart and had to look away from the tragic scene. Her eyes went to the bottles and the strange faces inside them. She put a hand over her mouth to cover her gasp as she saw Leroy's face appear inside a large bourbon bottle.

Iris put a finger to her lips as she pulled away from Vanessa.

She wasn't sure what she was going to do, but she knew she needed to get Leroy out of that bottle. Moving as quickly as she dared, she tried not to make a sound as she crossed the open dance floor.

Maybe it was the music or maybe it was his own weeping, but the man didn't hear her approach. With a quick jab forward, Iris pressed the taser to the center of his back.

He let out a startled cry and jerked violently before crumbling to the floor. Iris yelped just as loud, jerking back from him.

"Oh god, I did it!" she said to no one.

"Go Iris," Vanessa whisper-called. "What now?"

Holding up a hand, she called quietly back, "Stay there as lookout."

Iris glanced up and saw the woman in red kneeling by the unconscious necromancer. Their eyes met.

"I am sorry . . . I promise he is just knocked out!" she said to the woman in the mirror. "I just needed him out for a moment. He will be fine."

The woman looked skeptical as she petted the head of the man in the reflection.

"I am sorry, I have to free them," Iris said. The woman in red didn't respond as Iris hurried over and grabbed the bourbon bottle. She tried to peel off the wax cap, but it didn't budge.

"Leroy!" she called, holding the bottle up to her face to try and peer in. Like an old movie cliché, he sat on a barstool, smoking, a tumbler of bourbon in his hand, a half-empty bottle in front of him, his clothes rumpled and his eyes tired. He seemed to be talking to someone that Iris couldn't see. His smile was almost jagged, like the edge of broken glass. His eyes were bits of flint, hard and cold. Fear grabbed at Iris's heart. She didn't know what was happening to him in there, but she didn't like it. Without thinking, she slammed the bottle down on the hardwood. It shattered and she gasped as a rush of cold vapor flooded out of it. In the mirror, she watched as people stumbled out as if kicked out of the bar. Leroy fell to the floor next to her reflection. He heaved and retched, a green mist pouring out of his mouth.

"Leroy!" she yelled. "Are you alright?"

He coughed and looked up at her with a strange little smile. "Still dead, Dish, so that's aces." His grin was lopsided, and his eyes didn't focus.

Iris frowned. "Are you drunk?!"

He tried to shift his weight to stand but only got as far as a propped-up reclining pose.

"Oh, don't get sore, Doll. It was just a little sauce." He gave her his most charming smile.

"Oh boy . . ." Iris frowned and looked at the other bottles. "Well, it got you out of the bottle." Iris grabbed the next bottle and smashed it against the floor. The sound of shattering glass echoed in the dance hall. Again, a whoosh of vapor filled Iris's vision. People swirled into existence within the mirror. Some of them were as solid as Iris's own reflection. The rest were more like faded photographs or ethereal afterglows. Iris senses were muddled. Her connection to Leroy made the worlds blur as the green vapor floated through the dance hall.

Iris didn't stop; she grabbed another and another, trying to smash them as fast as she could.

She was only halfway through the bottles when a strong hand grabbed her wrist.

"No, you are killing her!"

The man in the hood had made it to his feet. He yanked Iris's arm hard, trying to pull the bottle away.

"Iris!" Vanessa shrieked, barely audible over the breaking of glass.

"She is already dead!" Iris shouted back, putting both hands on the bottle to hold on.

"You're wrong, I can save her! I will save my wife!" His eyes were wild, and she could hear desperation in his voice. It was so full of pain and fear that it made Iris pause. She looked up at his face and over his shoulder at the mirror behind him. It was a reflection of a room so crowded that the spirits overlapped each other, swirling in multicolored mist and vapor.

Iris couldn't find Leroy. It was so full she could barely see herself. Suddenly, the woman in red silently slammed against the inside of the mirror. She pounded her fists against it. Iris felt fear climb up her chest to choke her as she looked at the woman's face. She seemed to be staring directly into Iris's soul.

What is she doing? Why does she look so scared? What is she trying to say?

The red-dress woman waved her arms frantically, pointing her index finger directly at Iris.

Iris released the bottle and stood still in the center of the empty dance room. The man frantically put the bottle back into place. He started chanting in earnest. Iris continued to watch as the woman in red gestured wildly. Her mouth moved as she shouted but there was no sound.

She looks so scared. Was I hurting her?

The man in the hood knelt facing the mirror, still chanting.

Wait, she isn't pointing at me.

The broken glass littering the floor behind Iris crunched.

Iris flinched as the world went dark.

Chapter Twenty-Two

LEROY'S VISION swirled as he swayed. He was dancing. He could hear the music, but it was muffled by the cotton in his head. He smiled as he looked down to apologize to Iris.

That's not Iris. Her hair was the wrong color, a deep rich black, looking lovely against the blood-red dress. He tried to remember the name of the beautiful woman he was dancing with. They swirled around in the crowded room. She was looking up at him, her eyes a deep green. He should have been happy to dance with such a dish. Instead, he started looking around for a head of brown. His vision blurred and he stumbled again. He grabbed hold of the woman.

"Oh. I don't think I should be doing the jitterbug right now . . . Shit . . . my head."

The woman nodded, holding him up as she helped him towards the edge of the smoke.

Leroy leaned against the glass mirror and looked into the world of the living. His vision focused, and he saw Iris laying on the ground, surrounded by broken glass. Only a few feet away, two men were struggling. Vanessa was lying uncon-scious by the door.

The sounds became clearer. Spirits around him began to weep, scream, yell. Rage and fear filled the mists of the mirror, pressing in on him from all sides. The woman in red suddenly shoved Leroy hard. Pain ripped through him as he was pushed into the living world, the link to Iris giving him a tiny crack to slip through.

He moved and crouched down next to her. A large bruise was already forming on her pretty face. Leroy looked over as a man he had never seen before finally gained the upper hand over the necromancer.

The necromancer froze as the larger man pulled out a strangely shaped blade. It was almost the length of Leroy's forearm, and the outside curve was razor sharp while the inside was serrated. The necromancer's eyes went wide as the spirits screamed in terror. Shades and nightmares began to howl at the edges of the candlelight.

"Chad? You're the one that killed them?" The necromancer's voice was shocked, his face full of disbelief and fear.

"Interesting . . . What's with all this hocus pocus stuff? You trying to talk to your dead wife? Maybe, I will help you out." The knife bearer said in a strangely calm voice. Leroy felt a shiver run through him at the slightly amused tone he heard in that low timber. Moving around to get a better look at the man crouching over the cowering necromancer, Leroy felt anger rip through him as he saw a glint of the detective badge on the man's belt.

"A dirty cop . . . We should have guessed, Iris. That makes sense." Leroy spat at the man, but it had no effect. *Damnit, can't touch him.*

"I thought you were investigating me, Paul. You were taking all those unauthorized samples from the bodies." Chad laughed a little, waving the blade point towards Paul's face. The smaller man flinched back, eyes wide with fear, watching the point sway like a cobra head ready to strike.

Chad smirked, enjoying his game of fear. Leroy moved back towards Iris.

"Come on, Dollface, I need you to wake up." He crouched down and tried to shake her awake. He looked over at Vanessa. She was also crumpled on the floor by the door.

"I have been following you for a while. And then what do I see? This pair of hotties following you in, and this one has some of my missing property." Chad laughed and shook his head. "I thought you were working together until she zapped you!" He grinned maliciously. "I don't know what kind of twisted things you are into, but I have to say, I am digging the ambience. All these mirrors and soundproofing." He nodded as he pulled out a set of zip ties. "This is going to be fun."

Paul tried to get away, but the larger man put the blade to his throat, and he froze. Chad quickly tied Paul's hands.

"Don't move." Chad's voice was pleasant as he turned.

Leroy tried to attack Chad as he approached Iris.

"Don't touch her, you son of a bitch!" His fist passed uselessly through him. "Fuck," he shouted as panic filled him.

Chad reached down and grabbed Iris by her hair and pulled her roughly across the floor. Bits of glass left little slices on her face and arms. She groaned and whimpered as he pulled her over next to Paul.

"Leave her alone! She doesn't know anything," Paul said.

"Oh, she knows something, Paul. She found my little trophy stash. And I am going to find out how." He stepped away, dragged Vanessa in a similar way, and lined her up along with the rest of them. He caressed the knife up Iris's leg.

Paul kicked at him. "Chad, you fucking limp-dick son of

a bitch, you are a cop. You sick fuck. Don't you touch them!" He started thrashing and threw himself at Chad.

Leroy paced back and forth, helpless and furious. "Oh shit, Roy, this is a terrible plan."

He frowned as he rushed forward, pushing himself into Iris's unconscious body.

The world exploded around him. The flames of the candles burned like suns in the desert. The rhythmic thundering of his heart in his ears blocked out everything but the gasping rasp of his breathing. His skin felt as if he were burned and standing in a freezer. Every muscle and bone seemed to ache. His mouth was filled with a tang of copper from the blood. The right side of his face throbbed and ached. *I have to move . . . Move, damn it!*

He shouted over the noise, trying to focus through the chaos. He blinked and cleared his vision. Just visible through the glare of the candles he saw the two men fighting. Leroy threw his whole weight into the bodies tackling, curving his shoulder so that it would hit right into the side of the large man.

His shoulder made contact instead of moving through his target as he was used to. He slammed into a wall of flesh that felt like it was made of brick. The pain helped him focus, and he shook off some of the haze and noise. Leroy fell backwards and looked up, and up . . . *What the fuck . . . Did he grow? This guy must be like eight feet tall! He is huge!*

Chad turned and grinned, looking down at Leroy. He gave a wink and leaned towards him with a grotesque expression on his face.

"Hey there, little bitch. You think you can fight me?"

Leroy felt a sudden rush of fear and pain surge through him. He flashed back to his childhood when his father came at him drunk with a belt. The rage gave him strength and focus. His fist finally found his mark on the giant. The world exploded into pain as the large man stumbled under the surprisingly powerful blow.

Leroy also fell backwards, cradling his broken hand. "Shit . . . SHIT Fuck." He gasped, looking down to see the damage. The hit had been direct but too much. Three of the delicate fingers of the hand were either broken or dislocated. The soft, smooth knuckles were bruised and bleeding. The soft little hand just couldn't handle the force of the blow.

Leroy stared in horror. *That is not my hand!*

"NO, it's mine!" Iris screamed at Leroy.

The pain in her hand gave Iris the strength to push her way to the surface of consciousness. Leroy, remembering it was not his body, fell forward as he was ejected and Iris regained control.

Tears streamed down her face as she cradled her hand to her chest.

Leroy looked up and reached out a hand. "Sorry . . . Look out!"

"Fucking bitch, it's gonna be yours." Chad snarled in response to Iris, completely unaware of Leroy.

Iris let out another shriek as Chad tried to grab her. She twisted away wildly and scrambled across the floor.

Leroy lurched to his feet and looked around frantically. "Weapon. Get a weapon and hit the bastard!"

Adrenaline fueled Iris as she kicked Chad, deflecting him momentarily. Her eyes darted around the dim room. Her taser wasn't far off and the blade he had been carrying lay to the right. She barely heard Leroy over the noise of the room. Spirits were howling, men shouting, women weeping and screaming. The whole room was filled with the spirits of those Chad had wronged.

There are so many of them.

Iris felt the burning pain from her broken fingers and the sharp sting of all the broken glass cutting into her skin.

Leroy was still shouting to grab a weapon. "The knife, get the knife, it's right there, you can reach it!"

She finally spotted what she was looking for and threw herself forward. Using her uninjured hand, she stretched out grabbing the broken neck of the bourbon bottle. She felt it slice into her palm as she gripped it tight.

Chad finally managed to get ahold of her ankle, pulling her back through the broken glass. She screamed and struggled as he yanked her upright. *He is so strong.* Spinning her to face him, he gripped her by the neck and lifted her up, bringing their faces close together. She could feel his panting breath against her cheek. Her feet dangled, unable to find purchase on the floor.

Iris kicked and squirmed. She arched her spine trying to put any distance between them. She gripped the bottle neck tightly, waiting for the right moment. His smile grew, his eyes blazing.

"That's right, scream for me."

Iris felt bile rise in her throat. He leaned forward and licked blood and tears from her cheek. His eyes were hard and unfeeling. When he moved, his face closer again, she tried to bite him.

He jerked his head back, laughing. "So feisty. I love it."

Iris jabbed the broken bottle as hard as she could into his arm that was holding her by the neck. She felt the glass sink and splinter into the muscle and bone. He howled in pain and fury before he flung her across the room. She slammed into the mirror; she heard the crack.

Was that the glass or me?

In helpless desperation, Leroy had tried anything and everything he could to stop Chad. Shouting, attacking using every ounce of his spirit powers. He tried to push himself into anyone else's body, including Vanessa's. Anything that might be able to stop what was happening. Without the connection, he was unable to even bring them from unconsciousness.

Leroy saw Iris stab Chad with the bottle.

He watched Chad throw Iris against the mirror.

And then several things happened within the span of a few heartbeats.

Firstly, Iris broke the mirror, releasing the trapped spirits in an explosion of vapor. Secondly, Chad bled on the bottle, mingling his blood with Iris's. Thirdly, Chad looked up in surprise as he met Leroy's gaze.

"Who the fuck are you?" Chad snarled.

Leroy's lips curled into a vicious smile. "Where are my manners? Let me introduce myself." Leroy marched forward, plowing his fist into Chad's solar plexus. "I am Leroy Mahoney."

Chad's air left him in a pained rush as he folded, holding his stomach. Leroy's left hand cross connected with Chad's face. He crashed into what remained of the circle of bottles around the magic barrel.

"Private dick," Leroy said in a low voice.

The glass bottles shattered beneath Chad's weight, slicing painfully into his back. He snarled as he looked up at Leroy.

"You're fucking dead!" he shouted as he got to his feet.

Leroy's eyes glowed as he stepped forward and grasped the killer's shirt.

"You're not wrong." A quick right jab broke Chad's nose

with a gushing crunch. "But you've got no idea how right you are."

The next punch slammed Chad into the floor. His blood splattered across the hardwood and mixed with the liquid pouring out of the barrel.

Chapter Twenty-Three

Iris watched through a haze as the spirits suddenly went silent. Iris curled around herself, bringing her legs to her chest, trying to keep her warmth. Frost spread out around her. Her breath turned into a cloud of steam around her face. The world held its breath as all the shapes and shadows turned in unison towards the man on the floor.

Chad's eyes went wide, darting around as the figures became visible to him. Iris smiled even as her teeth chattered.

"Now they can reach you." Her whisper filled the silence of the room. Chad didn't even have a chance to scream. There was a feeling of rushing wind and an unearthly wail as the vapors swirled and poured themselves into Chad. They sucked all the magic with them, all but one candle going out. He convulsed and jerked on the floor, flopping and wiggling until finally, he was still.

Everything was still.

Iris felt the warmth return. She looked around and saw the woman in red kneeling next to the necromancer, petting him softly and kissing his brow. She flickered and wavered as the last candle slowly went out. The room fell into darkness.

After a stumbling, painful search, Iris was able to turn on the light. She dialed the police and sat down next to the still unconscious Vanessa.

She didn't see Leroy, but she wasn't worried. She knew he would be back.

Leroy winced as pain lanced through his temple in unison with Michael's fist slamming into the table. Leroy blinked, trying to clear his vision as Michael paced back and forth in the small interview room. Goldie watched from the far corner, smirking.

"Go over it again," Michael demanded.

"I can sing it louder if you want, but it's going to be the same song," Leroy grumbled.

"Leroy . . . Just do it," Jack said as he put a steaming cup in front of him.

Leroy tried not to let his irritation show and took a hold of the cup.

" . . . Like I said before, I was sitting in the cell one minute, and then next thing I know, a Shroud is dragging me to the land of the living." Leroy sipped gratefully from the warm brew. It helped ease some of his discomfort as the ragged edges of his essence refilled. One of the few perks of being dead: no lasting aches. Pain was either a flash in the pan or an eternal-fire kind.

"This necromancer, Paul, had more juice than he should have. He was operating a bootleg whiskey barrel. He trapped us in sealed glass bottles and then poured us into the barrel. From what I could figure out, in the barrel we fermented into something that his dead wife could drink."

Michael scoffed again, shaking his head. "Just as likely is

that you are making this all up to cover up the fact that you have been stealing soul energy all this time."

Leroy glared at Michael. "Maybe you're just looking for someone to take the fall for you sleeping on the job. You're a new kind of special. If I was going to make up a story, I would make sure it wasn't so embarrassing to tell."

Jack held up a hand between the two of them. "Easy gentleman. Easy."

Michael snarled, looking at Jack. "I don't believe him for a second. He is full of smooth, slick answers."

Leroy gave a caustic, almost feral grin as he looked at Michael. "Should I stutter?"

Michael lunged forward and was snatched away by Jack, who shoved him out of the room. The whole time Michael argued, "We both know he is hiding something. I bet he possessed this Paul and used him to consume the spirits. Lethal possessions are a ripping offense. You are done, Mahoney."

Leroy looked away, gripping his cup. His jaw was tight, and he had to take a moment to calm down. Michael wasn't wrong. Possessions were one of the highest offenses. If they figured out he had possessed Iris even for a minute, his goose would be cooked and served. The Wardens and arbiters had checked three times, trying to prove he had possessed Chad and caused his death.

"I am getting real tired of repeating myself, Jack."

Jackal nodded. "Then let us finish this," he said as he settled himself into a seat across from Leroy.

The men sat in silence for a moment. Leroy could feel the weight of the jackal's gaze. The pressure to confess every dark deed or questionable act. Everything that might make his heart heavy. He could feel the magic making the desire to put those burdens down stronger than ever before. He clenched his cup. *I have to give Jack something*. He clung on as long as he could.

Make it convincing, Leroy.

How to get through an interrogation: you start off with a spoonful of the "I don't know." Then a nice helping of "even if I did, I wouldn't tell you" And about the time it looks like someone might take a swing is when you bring out the main course. Mix up about half of what they already know, a quarter of bullshit, and a quarter of shit you don't want people to know.

For me, it's an easy recipe; I have plenty of both.

Leroy looked down at his steaming cup of energy, then drank down the last of its contents.

"I was a drunk, Jack. Working with Eugene was the only job I could hold down. But even half drunk, I was a damn fine PI. I spent half my time at the office, the other half in a bottle. That's why she was going to marry Eugene. I stepped into that dance hall and BAM . . . I was right back there. I could taste the bourbon on my tongue; I could smell the cigarette smoke. Like I was at my favorite spot."

Jack raised an eyebrow, a little surprised.

"Most people who suffer from an addiction have those tethers follow them into the afterlife."

Leroy nodded. "I had recently dried out. Had been since Eugene had proposed to her. Since he was going to be a novelist and a family man, I was going to take over the shop. Then I got fitted for my Chicago overcoat and he was writing about me in his books. He left out a few flaws. God bless him, he wrote a much better version of me."

Jack nodded and motioned for Leroy to continue.

"Anyways, inside the bottle was like being somewhere between a memory and a dream. It was so real. And while you are trapped there, it melts you down with the other people in the bottle. I must have been in with all the other drunks. It was a very crowded bar."

Leroy shook his head in disbelief. "If it hadn't been for the ditzy dame, I might not have made it out. I didn't even know I was trapped, but then—boom, crash, the world shatters. I get flung into a pocket-mirror world along with everyone else trapped in that bottle. Iris is smashing these bottles all over the place, and all these souls are being dumped into this little pocket. It felt like we were being pulled into the barrel in the center. Then, I see this woman in red. She is being fed from the central barrel."

Jack nodded. "Yes, we know all that. We have confirmed that the spirit barrel was designed to capture souls and feed them to a Spirit Ghoul. The Spirit Ghoul was the Necromancer's wife. He was attempting to use the ancient magical item to being her back. Now, if you would please answer the question we need to know. What happened after Iris smashed the bottle?"

Leroy grimaced as he thought about that moment. "It was a chaotic mess. I could barely follow what was happening. There was a man there, attacking both Iris and the necromancer. I kept trying to help Iris, but I couldn't even touch him. Suddenly, Iris uses one of the broken bottles to cut the guy. Which finally let my fist connect. So, I started wailing on the guy, and he fell right on top of the stupid barrel. Then bam, every spirit in the room is rushing him."

Jack tilted his head and looked behind Leroy at the wall. Leroy knew that was where the others were watching from.

"All he has said is truth."

Leroy smirked a bit and shook his head. "Sorry to disappoint. I know you all were hoping to hang this around my neck."

Jack tilted his head. "Did you see which spirits were involved in the attack on the living?"

Leroy shrugged. "Did you see which raindrop made my hat wet?"

Jack leaned forward. Leroy stiffened as that jackal muzzle came closer and opened slightly. Razor sharp fangs were visible as Jack whispered into his ear.

"This is a great number of loopholes you are dodging through. Take care they don't become a noose."

Leroy managed to keep his smirk in place, but the shiver made his hand twitch.

Threat or warning, he is right. I need to play it straight for a little while.

Leroy nodded and smiled. "You got it."

Jack shifted back and leaned in his chair. "So, tell me, Leroy, where is the girl?"

Leroy leaned back and shrugged. "I was hired to resolve her tether; you wanted me to find the lost souls." Leroy shrugged. "I found the stolen souls. The tether is resolved; the girl can move on now. Maybe you should do the same."

The right ear on Jack's head twitched. His dark muzzle huffed in annoyance as he shook his head slightly.

"I have no other questions. You may leave."

Leroy nodded, getting his coat and hat. "Have a nice day. See ya around, Jack."

Jack's response was an irritated growl as Leroy closed the door behind himself.

Leroy whistled all the way back to his office. Frankie was at the front desk. He looked the same as always, stick thin and wearing a checkered vest and suit. His hair was slicked down and parted on the left side. He jumped to his feet.

"Leroy! I haven't seen you in days. Are you ok? I was worried." Frankie sounded as shaky as ever.

Leroy grinned at him. "Yeah, I am aces. Sorry I wasn't

able to check in. It's all settled now, so don't worry. Why don't you take the rest of the day off?"

Frankie gave a little smile. "Are you sure? I can stick around if you need me."

Leroy laughed and patted him on the shoulder. "You're a pal. But I just need some peace and quiet while I prop my feet up and take a breather."

Frankie nodded. "You got it, boss." He grabbed his coat and hat. Turning the sign to closed, he shut the door behind himself.

Leroy headed to his desk and looked around. Mouse was sitting in Eugene's chair with her feet propped up on the desk.

Leroy jumped in surprise. "SHIT! Mouse, you scared me half to death."

Mouse laughed as she put her feet back to the floor. "That would be quite the trick since you are already dead."

Leroy frowned as he rested against the side of his desk. "Where the hell have you been? I could have used some help."

Mouse sighed. "Those are the rules. I am not allowed to interfere once the Fates are called. I came back as soon as I was able. I wanted to be sure to say goodbye to Lucy."

Leroy raised an eyebrow. "Considering all the trouble that I am in, I should only have to pay half price."

Mouse laughed and shrugged. "It costs what it costs. Besides, if it weren't for that Iris lady, you both would still be stuck in that bourbon bottle. You were lucky to have been able to grab Lucy before you were sucked in."

Leroy gave Mouse a cheeky grin. "Oh, so you were watching. Did you help with that bit of luck?"

Mouse crossed her arms. "You are not as charming as you think you are. I couldn't interfere with you. But Lucy wasn't a part of the roll. I was free to help her. Speaking of which, I believe she has waited long enough."

Leroy made sure the office door was locked tight before he pulled Lucy out of his magic coat pocket.

She blinked in the light and looked around.

"Leroy!" she said as she threw her arms around him. Mouse smiled as she watched them.

He let out a relieved sigh and hugged her tight. "It's alright, Kid. You're alright now."

Lucy sniffled and cried for a moment while he patted her back.

"Alright, alright. Enough with the waterworks."

It took her a moment, but she nodded and wiped her face. "Miss Mouse!" Mouse and Lucy exchanged a tight hug. "You found me." Lucy gave them both a soft smile.

"Oh yes, Roy was very worried about you. He moved the very Fates to find you," Mouse said, wearing a big smile.

Leroy rubbed at the back of his neck in embarrassment. "Well, I had a job to do. And Leroy Mahoney always finishes the job."

He pulled the small gold locket out of his pocket and slowly lowered it into Lucy's hands. Her face lit up, happiness literally increasing the glow on her cheeks.

"You got it back!"

He grinned and nodded. "Of course I did."

Lucy held it close to her heart and smiled. "Does this mean I can find my mamma now?"

Leroy nodded slowly and smoothed the hair on the top of her head. Mouse smiled, watching the moment silently.

"That's right, Kiddo, you should be able to cross over, no problem."

Lucy looked between them. "How do I do that?"

Leroy laughed and shrugged. "Well, I am not an expert there. Some folks say it's seeing a light or the face of a loved one. It's different for everyone. I would try calling your mom first."

Mouse nodded her agreement. "Yeah, I think that would be the best thing to try first."

Lucy looked very serious, concentrating as she closed her eyes.

"Mom! Mamma!" she tried calling out a few times. Lucy was very still for a moment then gasped in surprise. She turned to her right, responding to something only she could hear. "MAMMA!" she shouted in excitement and took off running. She disappeared in a flash of rainbow sparkles and glittering butterflies.

They fluttered around the room before landing and turning into glowing bits of spiritual energy. Mouse reached out and scooped up a large handful. She carefully put it into a little pouch where she kept her drasis.

"Good travels, Lucky Little Lucy," Mouse whispered into the glowing dust.

Leroy blinked against the bright lights. He wiped at his eyes, pretending he didn't notice the moisture there. He smiled when he saw the small sunflower barrette sitting in a pile of the raw energy on the floor. He picked it up and tucked it away in his pocket for safekeeping.

Mouse smiled and nodded. "I will be seeing you, Roy." She swirled away in a soft cloud of blue dust.

"Not if I see you first." Leroy chuckled as he scooped up a handful of the drasis. It turned into coins in his hand. He tucked those away into his pocket. The rest of the glittering dust absorbed slowly into his office and the world around him.

With a satisfied sigh, he walked over and sat down in his chair. He leaned back, put his feet up on his desk, pulled a cigarette from his case, flicked a match, lit it, and took a long drag.

He normally would have smoked at the window, but he wanted to stretch out his legs. After his second drag, he tilted his hat over his eyes and let his head fall back. But he couldn't stop the nagging feeling in the back of his mind. He tried to ignore it, but there was something itching in his brain.

What am I forgetting?

He must have been tired because it took him almost the entire smoke to recall. His feet thumped to the floor as he stood back up.

"Oh shit . . . It's a good thing I am already dead, or Iris would kill me."

He grabbed his coat and headed back out the door.

Chapter Twenty-Four

IRIS WAS WONDERING, and not for the first time, if there was a way to bring Leroy back from the dead . . . so she could murder him. *I understand why someone might have put a hex on him in the first place.*

An EMT had suggested to the detectives that she go to a hospital. He had done the bandages of her deeper cuts and treated the smaller ones. He had also warned of a concussion, and she had been stuck in this interrogation room ever since. She was tired, thirsty, and she had to pee.

Iris had told her story four different times, told it forwards, backwards, and sideways. But she was good at keeping a lie straight. Iris didn't want to call her lawyer because he would report back to her father. *If I don't get to pee soon, I am going to call anyway.*

A new detective walked in. This would be the fifth one she had spoken to. So far, she had been interviewed by three women and now this was the second man. The women had tried to be friendly, sympathetic, and even bitchy. The first male detective had tried to be very aggressive and forceful in tone.

"

But Iris had spent too much time dealing with people of extreme wealth and privilege. She wasn't going to crack with so little pressure. Most people don't understand how ruthless the elitist assholes can be. Iris realized this was a higher-ranking detective because he wore a more expensive suit.

"Miss Porterfield. Thank you for your patience. We appreciate it. I just want to ask a few more questions if you don't mind."

Iris looked up at him. She could tell her face was swollen and her glasses were cracked.

"Actually, I do mind. I do not wish to answer any further questions."

Up until this point, she had been very helpful. Iris knew that the lower-ranking officers didn't decide when she went home. They had to stall because they couldn't make the decision. That was the job of a lieutenant or above. Now that he was here, it was time to start playing hard ball.

He seemed a little surprised by her polite but firm statement.

"I have been more than patient with this process, but in the last forty-eight hours I have been attacked twice, shot and terrorized. I am injured, I am in pain. I am the victim here. You and your detectives have been treating me like a suspect. Now, I think I am done with questions for the evening. I would like to go to the hospital. I want to know if my friend Vanessa is ok."

He looked serious and sat down, not responding. "Miss Porterfield, this will all go a lot easier if we can just understand what happened tonight. There are a lot of blank areas we need to clarify here. If we can just get through this, all can be settled, and we can move on."

Iris gave him a withering look. "It is not my job to fill in the blanks for you, Detective. I will, however, give you five more minutes, and then I am leaving to go to the hospital. If anyone dislikes that, then I will be contacting my attorney."

The lieutenant's eyes narrowed. He knew a threat when he heard one. "Why would you need an attorney if you have done nothing wrong, Miss Porterfield?" His voice lowered a half octave.

Iris looked down at her phone. "I wouldn't waste your five minutes on that question."

He stiffened and leaned forward. "Alright, then how about you explain why you were in the building?"

Iris sighed, making a show of how annoyed she was. "As I have said to every officer before you, Vanessa and I were on a walk, and we heard a shout from inside. We thought someone was calling for help. The door was open, so we went inside."

"That was brave of you, considering it was just you two ladies. Weren't you afraid?"

Iris glared at him. Real anger bubbled to the surface. "Wow, just blatant sexism now. Interesting choice. Is this where you start asking me if I had been drinking? Or if we were meeting a man? Did you want to measure my skirt?" Iris lost ahold of her anger. She was so sick of this stupidity. "Or maybe this is because he was a cop. You are trying to blame me and my friend. You are trying to protect him?! I am the one he planned on raping and murdering. You know how I knew he was going to do that? Because he fucking told me! And you are sitting here, acting like I was asking for it." She snatched up her phone. "You know what, I changed my fucking mind. I am done." She hit the speed dial right in front of the detective, who was doing his best to maintain his cool. His face was flushing red.

The phone was answered by the second ring. Her family lawyer was on the line less than two minutes later.

In less than ten minutes, a female detective was escorting

Iris and Vanessa out of the station and to the hospital. She was seen to directly, and her clothes were taken into evidence. She was swabbed and her wounds photographed. Vanessa and Iris were back at the office a bit after midnight.

The two women hugged and curled up together on the couch with the TV playing. Bogart watched over them until the sun filtered through the window curtains.

Iris got up to put on the coffee. Vanessa sighed and stood up.

"Will you please sit down? You look terrible. Please let someone look after you a little bit. Your hand is broken, for god's sake. I still can't believe it took them that long to get you to the hospital."

Iris nodded and slowly sank down into the seat. Everything hurt even more than it had yesterday. Her hand throbbed. Her head ached, and the slash and all the little cuts from the broken glass on her arm burned and throbbed when she moved too much.

"This is going to make work very difficult."

"What kinda dame worries about work when she barely survived the night before?" Leroy said as he appeared by the window. Iris gasped, a little startled.

"What is it?" Vanessa asked. "Oh, is it your ghost boyfriend?"

Iris wanted to give Vanessa a look, but her face hurt so she just glared at Leroy.

"What took you so long?" she said, irritated.

"Don't flip your wig; I had things to deal with. I was being grilled by the Wardens, which are basically ghost cops. Then I had to deal with Mouse and Lucy," he said as he stepped forward. He flinched and frowned as he looked at Iris's face. "Oh, that's a serious shiner. Sorry about the hand, Doll."

Iris huffed and shook her head. "I still can't believe you did that. I don't know what kind of girl you think I am, but I don't just let men inside me."

Vanessa snickered from the sink. She called back, "From what you described, he wasn't in there that long . . .," then under her breath she mumbled, "which was still longer than Brenden."

Leroy couldn't suppress a chuckle. He cleared his throat and had the decency to look sheepish at Iris's red face.

"I know you're not that kinda gal. I am sorry." He frowned and looked over her injuries. "How's your hand?"

She held up her fresh cast. "You broke a bunch of little bones. But I should make a full recovery."

"That's good." He sighed and sat down in the chair across from her. "I just wanted to tell you that the kid made it back to her mom. And you freed a lot of trapped souls. You saved us, Iris. And you stopped a killer. I know the cops hassled you, and no one is ever going to read about it in the papers. But you're a hero, a real Wonder Woman."

Iris blushed under the praise and smiled a little to herself. That hurt a bit, but she did it anyway. "Thank you for telling me. I am glad I was able to help." She shifted in her seat.

Vanessa smirked as she looked over at Iris. She didn't have to hear what Leroy was saying, she could tell by the look on Iris's face. Iris got that same smile anytime someone told her she had done a good job.

Vanessa started getting things together to cook breakfast while the coffee brewed.

Leroy sat fiddling with his hat. He frowned at himself. He knew he had to take the anchor out. When he did, she wouldn't see or hear him; he wouldn't see her like this anymore.

"Well, I just wanted to let you know. So, thanks for the help, and just like I promised, I will take out the anchor and you will be back to normal."

He didn't move and just continued to play with his hat.

Iris nodded and fussed with her pajamas. "Well, that's good, normal is good. There has been way more excitement than I need."

Leroy nodded and let out a laugh. "That's right . . ."

They both laughed a little as they stalled.

Finally, Leroy forced himself to his feet. "Well, be seeing you, Doll," he said as he reached out to pull the anchor free.

When he felt the magic release, he stepped back and put his hat on his head. Iris watched him with a serious face. Turning away from her, he knew she would slowly disappear as he lost his connection to the living world.

Leroy didn't look at her. He didn't want to watch her fade away. He felt a clenching pain in his chest. His face was set in a hard line as he tried to ignore the sense of loss. He felt the emptiness of his office and tried to ignore how he felt.

It's for the best . . . She has a long life ahead . . . She doesn't need someone like me hanging around and messing it all—

"Is something supposed to happen?" Iris asked.

Leroy whipped around in shock.

She was still sitting right there. He checked and the line was gone, but somehow, the connection remained.

Iris blinked and looked concerned. "Leroy . . . you look like you have seen a ghost . . . Or at least a ghost that actually scares you."

Leroy frowned. "It didn't work . . ."

Iris blinked, confused. "What do you mean, it didn't work."

Leroy waved a hand between them, "I took back the anchor, but you are still connected. I don't know why."

Iris frowned and shifted slowly forward. "But what does that mean?"

Leroy shook his head. "I don't know, Dollface, but we will be stuck with each other until we figure out how to break the connection."

Vanessa frowned. "What didn't work?"

Iris looked over at her and sighed. "It looks like Leroy can't break the connection, so I am still seeing ghosts."

Vanessa nodded. "Oh, well that makes sense if you think about it. I mean, you did see ghosts when we were kids. So maybe it's because of that. Anyway, did you want toast with your eggs?"

"What? You saw ghosts before now?" Leroy snapped his attention between Vanessa and Iris.

Iris nodded at Leroy but turned to answer Vanessa. "Yes, two pieces please. Thank you for making breakfast."

Leroy didn't understand how these two could be so calm. "Iris, this is serious, we could be stuck like this for a long time."

Iris smiled and nodded. "Yes Leroy, that's true, but I am sure we will figure it out. But for now, I need breakfast and rest."

Vanessa was setting plates at the table. "What is he saying?"

Iris gave a little laugh. "He is worried that we might be stuck this way for a while."

"Personally, I am relieved," Vanessa said as she set the coffees down, and Iris moved to the table slowly.

Iris looked up at Vanessa with a curious expression. "You mean for some other reason than I am not crazy?"

Vanessa laughed. "I never thought you were. I was referring to the fact that some strange men came in here and attacked you. They are still out there. And we still don't know what it was they were after. It's good to have some help figuring that out and keeping us safe."

Iris smiled up at the other woman. "Have I mentioned that you are awesome, Vanessa?"

Vanessa beamed and nodded. "That is correct and don't forget it. Now, eat your eggs."

Leroy looked at the two women with a kind of dismayed respect. *Women these days are terrifying.*

Leroy let out a sigh as he sat on his windowsill. Taking a long drag, he tried to calm his nerves. He couldn't deny that he was relieved that he wasn't losing Iris yet, but a deep worry filled him. It wasn't supposed to work this way. He would need to figure out what was happening and how to fix it.

He would need to find Mouse and ask her what was going on.

He had a distinct impression he wasn't going to like whatever she had to say.

"Women are going to be the death of me," he muttered.

Iris snickered from her seat. "Maybe they already were." She took a big bite of her toast.

Leroy did his best to not laugh too hard as he blew smoke out the window.

The End

About the Author

Jesse M. Harvey debut book is 'Motherhood at the End of the World.' She writes many types of fiction, including science fiction, space fantasy, supernatural, thriller and mystery. She graduated from Syracuse University with a Bachelor's degree in history

Jesse currently lives in Syracuse NY. She is married with three school age children. Her family comes from a military background, and her husband is a veteran.

Through all her work, Jesse includes underlying themes of hope, compassion, courage and determination. She believes that fiction shapes the future. Jesse wants to help inspire a more diverse and inclusive world.

https://jessemharveybooks.wordpress.com/

Also by Jesse M. Harvey

Motherhood at the End of the World

The Dark Stellar Series:

Scythia Protostar: Book One

Uthraith Tauristar: Book Two

The Dead Detective Series:

The Barrel Full of Spirits